the
hot spot

Other titles available in Vintage Crime/Black Lizard

By Jim Thompson

After Dark, My Sweet
The Getaway
The Grifters
A Hell of a Woman
Pop. 1280

By Charles Willeford

The Burnt Orange Heresy
Pick-Up

By David Goodis

Black Friday
Shoot the Piano Player

Also by Charles Williams

Man on a Leash

And the Deep Blue Sea

The Wrong Venus

Dead Calm

The Long Saturday Night

Aground

Man on the Run

All the Way

Talk of the Town

Uncle Sagamore and His Girls

Girl Out Back

The Diamond Bikini

The Big Bite

Scorpion Reef

A Touch of Death

Go Home Stranger

Nothing in Her Way

River Girl

Big City Girl

Hill Girl

The Sailcloth Shroud

the
hot spot

charles williams

VINTAGE CRIME / **BLACK LIZARD**

vintage books • a division of random house, inc. • new york

First Vintage Crime/Black Lizard Edition, October 1990

ISBN: 0-679-73329-9
Library of Congress Catalog Card Number: 90-50441

Manufactured in the United States of America
10 9 8 7 6 5 4 3 2

the
hot spot

1

THE FIRST MORNING when I showed up on the lot he called me into the office and wanted me to go out in the country somewhere and repossess a car.

"I'm tired of fooling with that bird," he said. "So don't take any argument. Bring the car in. Miss Harper'll go with you and drive the other one back."

I was working on commission, and there wasn't any percentage in that kind of stuff. I'd just started to tell him to get somebody else to run his errands when I saw the girl come in and changed my mind.

He introduced us. "Miss Harper," he grunted, shuffling through the papers on his desk. "Madox is the new salesman."

"How do you do?" I said. She was cool in summer cotton and had very round arms, just slightly tanned, and somehow she made you think of a long-stemmed yellow rose.

She nodded and smiled, but when he told her about going with me to pick up the car I could see she didn't like it.

"Can't we wait a little?" she asked doubtfully. "I think I can collect those back payments. I did once before. Let me go out and talk to Mr. Sutton myself."

He gestured curtly with the cigar. "Forget it, Gloria. We've got more to do than chase him all over hell every month to get our money. Bring in the car."

We took a '50 Chevvy off the lot and started out. I drove. "You'll have to tell me where," I said.

"Straight through town and south on the highway."

The business district was only one street about three blocks long. There was a cotton gin beyond that, and a

3

railroad station, with the tracks shining in the sun. It was just nine o'clock, but it was a bright, still morning with the smell of pine and hot pavement in the air.

She was very quiet. I turned and looked at her. She was sitting in the corner of the seat staring moodily at the road and the breeze set up by the car riffled gently through her hair. Any way you tried to describe the hair itself would make it sound like a thatched roof instead of the way it really looked. Maybe it was because it was so straight and wasn't parted anywhere. It was the colour of honey or of straw, with sun-burned streaks in it, and flowed down from the top of her head in a short bob with a kind of football helmet effect and on to her forehead with a V-shaped bang or whatever you call it. Her face was the same golden tan as her arms, and while I couldn't see her eyes very well, I remembered the impression when we were introduced of an almost startling violet splashed into all those shades of honey.

"Cigarette?" I asked.

She took one. "Thank you," she said. Her manner was friendly enough, but I could see something was bothering her.

"What's with this repossession deal?" I asked. "He carry his own financing on the cars he sells?"

"Yes. He's actually in the loan business. He just added the used-car lot the last year or so. Did you see that building right across the street from the lot, the Southland Loan Company? That's Mr. Harshaw's."

"And you work in the loan office—is that it?" I hadn't seen her around the lot yesterday when I got the job.

She nodded. "I run it for him. Most of the time, that is."

"I see."

We were silent for a moment, and then she asked, "Where are you from, Mr. Madox?"

"Me? Oh, I'm from New Orleans." It would do as well as any.

We hit the highway and went on down it for another ten miles. There were heavy stands of timber along here, and

not much farming land. I remembered from driving up
yesterday that it shouldn't be too far now to the long highway bridge over the river. We turned off to the right before
we got to it, though, taking a dirt road which led uphill
through heavy pine. At the top there were a couple of
farms, abandoned now, their yards grown up with weeds
and bullnettles and the unpainted buildings staring
vacantly at the road. The land began to drop away on the
west side of the ridge and then we were in the river bottom,
driving under big oaks, and it was a little cooler. Most of
the sloughs were dried up now, in midsummer, and when
we came out to the river itself it was low, with the sandbars
showing, and fairly clear. After we crossed it, I stopped the
car and got out and went back to stand on the end of the
wooden bridge looking at it.

It was beautiful. The river came around a long bend
above and slid over a bar into the big pool under the
bridge. Part of the pool was in the shadow of the dense wall
of trees along the bank and it looked dark and cool and
deep. The only sound anywhere was a mockingbird prac-
tising his scales from a pin oak along the other bank. There
was a peace here you could almost feel, like a hand touching you.

I went back to the car. As I got in she glanced at me
questioningly. "Why did you stop?" she asked.

"I don't know. I just wanted to look at it."

"It's pretty, isn't it? And peaceful."

"Yeah," I said.

I started the car. We went on across the bottom and up a
sandy road through more timber on another hill.

"Who is this guy Sutton?" I asked. "A hermit? The car
must have been worn out before he got home with it."

She came out of her moody silence. "Oh. He's the watchman at a well they started to drill back in here."

"Watchman?" I asked. "Are they afraid somebody'll steal
a hole in the ground?"

"No. You see, it's an oil well, and all the equipment is
still over here. Tools, and things like that. They started it
over a year ago and then there was some kind of lawsuit

which stopped everything. Mr. Sutton lives on the place to look after it."

"Do you know him? If he's got a job, why doesn't he pay off his car notes?"

She was looking down at her hands. "I just know him when I see him. He's been around here about a year, I guess. He doesn't come to town much, though."

For some reason she seemed to be growing more nervous. Once or twice she started to say something and never did quite get it out.

"What is it?" I asked.

"Well, not anything, really," she said uncomfortably. "I was just thinking it might be better if you let me talk to him. You see, he's—well, in a way he's kind of a hard man to deal with, and suspicious of strangers. He knows me, and maybe he'll listen to me."

"What does he have to listen to? We just take the car. That's simple enough."

"Well, I just thought perhaps—I mean, I might be able to get him to pay and we wouldn't have to take the car."

I shrugged. "It's O.K. with me." It wasn't any of my business. I was supposed to be selling cars, not collecting for them.

We went on a mile or so across the second ridge and then came abruptly to the end of the road. Across the clearing a derrick climbed above the dark line of trees behind it and on this side a rough frame shack roofed with tar paper was huddled against the overhanging oaks. The car, a '54 Ford, stood in the open near the small front porch. I stopped and we got out. Both the front and rear doors of the shack were open and we could see right through it to the timber beyond, but there was no one around nor any sound of life.

"He must be home," she said. "The car is here."

We walked over and stood before the porch. "Mr. Sutton," she called out tentatively. "Oh, Mr. Sutton." There was no answer.

I stepped up on the porch and went inside, but there was no one there. It was only one room, untidy—but not dirty— as if a man lived there alone, with a wood cookstove in one corner and an unmade three-quarter bed in the corner diagonally across from it. A kitchen table with dirty dishes still on it stood by the rear door, and clothing—mostly overalls and blue shirts—hung from nails driven into the walls. An armful of magazines lay stacked against the wall and two or three more were scattered on the bed. There was an ash-tray made of the lid of a coffee-can perched on the window ledge, and as my eyes swung past it, they stopped suddenly. About half the butts were smeared with lipstick. She hadn't said he was married. Well, I thought, maybe he's not.

I heard a step on the porch and turned. She had come in and was looking at me a little apprehensively. "Do you think we ought to come in like this when he's not here?" she asked. I kept getting the impression she was scared of him.

"I don't know," I said. "Maybe not. Say, is he married?" She shook her head. "I don't think so."

She saw the ash-tray then and looked away from me. I watched her as she kept glancing nervously around and it was obvious she didn't like the idea of our being in here. We went back outside. I walked out to the car and hit the horn-button three or four long blasts. Sound rolled out across the timber and then died away while we listened. There was no answer.

A small shed stood beside the derrick platform, over across the clearing, but from here we could see that the door was locked and he wasn't anywhere around it. At the side of the shack a trail led down into a wooded ravine, and when she saw me looking down that way she said, "He might be down at the spring where he gets his water. I'll walk down and see."

"All right," I said, starting to go with her.

"It's all right," she protested. "I'll go. Why don't you just wait by the car?"

I started to say something, and then shut up. For some reason she didn't want me to go. Maybe she was afraid of me. I've got a homely, beat-up face, and I'm pretty big.

"O.K.," I said. I sat down on the side of the porch and

lighted a cigarette. She went down the trail. I could catch only glimpses now and then of the blonde head and the crisp blue of her dress, and then she went out of sight around a turn. I waited, smoking, and wondering what she was nervous about. When I looked again she was halfway up the trail, coming back. I watched her, thinking how it would be, the way you always do, and how pretty she was. She was a little over average height and had a lovely walk, even in the flat sandals, and there was something oddly serious about her face, more so than you'd expect in a girl who couldn't be over twenty-one. She looked like someone who could get hurt, and it was strange I thought about it that way because it had been a long time since I'd known anyone who was vulnerable to much of anything. Her legs were long and very nice, and she wore rather dark nylons.

I stood up. "We might as well go," I said. "He may not be back all day."

"Oh," she said. "I found him. He was down at the spring."

I probably stared at her. She hadn't been out of sight more than two or three minutes. And why hadn't he come back with her?

"Did you get the car keys?" I asked.

She didn't look at me. "No. He paid me. Both payments. We won't have to take it."

I shook my head. "You must be a fast talker," I said. "I'm glad I don't owe you any money."

She turned towards the car. "Oh, he'd been intending to pay it. He just hadn't been to town. Hadn't we better go?"

"I guess so," I said. The whole thing was queer, but if he'd paid her there was no use hanging around.

We had just reached the car and were starting to get in when I looked up and saw the man walking towards us. He had come out of the trees on the road we had come in on, and was carrying a gun which looked like a .22 pump in the crook of his arm. She saw him, too. Her eyes were uneasy and when she glanced quickly sidewise at me, I knew it was Sutton and that she had been lying when she said she'd seen him down at the spring.

2

HE WAS A big man, around six feet and heavy all the way up, and walked with a peculiar short stride which some people might have called mincing but wasn't. It was the flat-footed shuffle of a bear or a heavyweight fighter, and men who move that way are balanced and hard to push off their feet. He was dressed in bib overalls and a faded blue shirt, and besides the gun he was carrying two fox squirrels by their tails. He appeared to be around thirty-five or thirty-eight, with a stubble of dark beard on an unlined, moon-shaped face, and he had the expression in his eyes of a man enjoying some secret and very dirty joke.

"Hello," I said.

He came up and stopped, glancing from Gloria Harper to me and back again. "Hello. You boys looking for some-body?"

"Yeah," I said. "A man named Sutton. Would that be you?"

"You've got me, men. What can I do for you?"

Before I could say anything she spoke up hurriedly. "It's about the car, Mr. Sutton. I—I mean could I talk to you for a minute?"

I waited to see what was going to happen next. She'd already told me he had paid up, which was obviously im-possible, so what was she going to do? I could feel her begging me not to say anything.

He turned and looked at her again. "Why, you sure can, honey." He was affable and co-operative, while the grin he gave her was crawling with that secret joke of his. It was edged with something like contempt and left her standing there naked and hot-faced and without any pride at all.

Her eyes were miserable and they begged "Please," as she looked towards me and then turned to walk to the shack with him. I leaned against the door of the car and watched them. He sat down on the porch and left her standing and took out a cigarette without offering her one. Just the way he sat there and watched her was a slap in the face, full of calculated insolence and that dirty humour of his. I couldn't hear what she was saying, but he was apparently enjoying it.

In a minute she turned away from him and came back to the car. Her face was still crimson and she avoided looking at me. "We can go now," she said.

"What about the car?"

"It's all right. We don't have to take it."

"He didn't pay you anything. What are you going to tell Harshaw?"

"Please," she said. She was very near to crying.

"O.K.," I said, and we got in. It was her funeral. She ran the loan office and it was her business and Harshaw's, not mine. I backed up and turned the car into the road while Sutton watched us from the porch and grinned.

We were almost back to the river before she said anything. "Maybe I'd better tell him," she said hesitantly. "Mr. Harshaw, I mean."

"It's your baby," I said. "Tell him anything you want."

"I—I know it must look a little funny, Mr. Madox."

"Is Sutton a relative of yours?"

"No."

"Well, a hundred and ten dollars is a lot of money."

She glanced at me and said nothing. She either had to pay those two car notes herself or juggle the books to make it look as if they'd been paid, and she knew that I knew it. When we came to the bridge over the river I pulled off the road under the trees and stopped. She didn't say a word, but when I turned to her, she was watching me a little uneasily. I put my arm around her and bent her head back. She didn't struggle or try to slap me. She didn't do anything. It was like kissing a passed-out drunk. I let go and she drew away from me as far as she could. She didn't look at me. I put a hand under her chin and turned it.

"Get with it, kid," I said. "Sutton sent me."

I could see the shame and distaste in her eyes. "You must be proud of yourself."

"We could still go back and repossess the car," I said.

She didn't answer.

"Or we could go in and tell Harshaw he wouldn't let us have it. That ought to be good for a laugh."

"Why are you doing this?"

"You never get anywhere if you don't try."

"Well, would you mind driving on, or shall I get out?"

"You're a cute kid. How old are you?"

"Twenty-one."

"Why're you afraid of Sutton?"

She blushed and looked out the window. "I'm not."

"Cut it out, blondie. How'd he get on your back?"

"It's—it's nothing. You're just imagining it."

"The way you imagined you saw him down at the spring? And collected the car notes?"

"All right, all right," she said desperately. "I lied about it. But why can't you leave me alone?"

"When I see something being passed around I like to get my share. I'm just a pig that way."

Her shoulders slumped and she looked down at her feet. "Well, now that you've expressed your opinion of me, could we go on to town?"

"What's your hurry? We're just getting acquainted. And besides, you haven't taken care of my car payments yet."

"I don't know what you're talking about."

"You, angel. Did I tell you that you had nice legs?" I started to go on from there, but she brushed the skirt down and shoved away and finally she did hit me. "O.K.," I said. "You don't have to call the Marines. I can take a hint." I switched on the ignition and turned the car back on the road. She was silent all the way back to town, just sitting in the corner of the seat rolling her handkerchief into a ball in her hands.

It was easy to see something was wrong before we got

there. A column of black smoke climbed straight into the sky from somewhere in town and a highway patrol car came boiling up behind us and careened past with its siren howling. I hit the accelerator and fell in behind it, wondering where the fire was and hoping it wasn't the rooming house I'd moved into yesterday.

It wasn't. It was a greasy-spoon hamburger shack beyond the cotton gin on the other side of the street. Smoke, red-laced with flame, boiled out of the rear door and the window while the front of the place was a traffic jam of men trying to get in with hoses and other men trying to fight their way out with tables and chairs and a big jukebox. The street was blocked with swollen white hoses and the one piece of fire-fighting equipment, an old pumper left over from the 'Twenties, while volunteer firemen ran back and forth carrying axes and yelling at each other. I slowed down, trying to get a better look, but the highway cop waved me on with a furious gesture of his arms, shouting something I couldn't hear above the uproar and pointing to the cross street detouring around the block.

I went up a couple of blocks and then turned back to the main street again, past the corner where the bank was. It was deserted here. Everybody was down at the other end fighting the fire or just gawking and getting in the way. When I turned in at the lot the other salesman was gone and Harshaw was alone in the office. As I got out I looked at her, wondering if she was going to say anything, but the big eyes were stony and blank, not even seeing me. She was probably scared blue of what I might say to Harshaw but she'd die before she'd plead again. She was a sweet-looking kid taking a beating about something, and suddenly I was ashamed and wanted to apologize.

"Wait——" I started. She turned her head and looked at me as if I were something crawling out of a cesspool and went on into the office with her back straight.

Harshaw was on the phone when I came in and she was waiting to talk to him. He hung up in a minute and looked across at me.

"You get the car?" he asked.

"No," I said. I sat down and lighted a cigarette.

"Why not?"

He had a habit of barking like a non-com, and he looked like one, like an old master sergeant with thirty years in. He was stocky and square-faced, around fifty-five, with a mop of iron grey hair, and the frosty grey eyes bored into you from under bushy overhanging brows. There were little tufts of hair in his ears, and he always had a cigar clamped in his mouth or in his hand.

I don't know why I did it. "Because he paid Miss Harper," I said.

He grunted. "Just have to do it again next month. The guy's a dead-beat. What's afire down there? The gin?"

"No. Hamburger joint across from it."

"Well, how about hanging around while I go to dinner?"

That burned me a little. I'd wasted the whole morning running an errand for him and now he wanted me to wait around while he went to eat. I got up from the table and started to the door. "Sure," I said. "As soon as I get back from mine."

He glared at me. "Maybe you won't like this job."

"That's right," I said. "Maybe I won't."

I went out, and as I started angling across the street she caught up with me, headed for the loan office. She walked alongside, not looking up, and when I glanced around at her the top of that blonde strawstack was just on a level with my eyes.

"Thank you," she said quietly.

"Forget it." I turned at the kerb and went on up the sidewalk.

Down the street I could see the smoke still boiling into the sky and the jam of cars and people around the fire engine. The restaurant was deserted, like everything else in this end of town, and when I sat down at the counter the lone waitress hurried up eagerly.

"Are they going to save it?" she asked.

"I don't know," I said. "I haven't been down there. How'd it start?"

"Somebody said a grease fire in the kitchen."

"Oh. Well, how's the grease here? You got a menu?"

She shook her head. "The dinner's not ready. Cook's gone to the fire. I could fix you a sandwich, though."

"Never mind," I said. "Just a glass of milk and a piece of pie."

It was awful pie and the crust was like damp cardboard. I wasn't hungry anyway, because of the heat, and I kept thinking about the girl and the whole crazy thing out there at the oil well. Why was she taking the responsibility for Sutton's car payments, and why had he looked at her that way? He hadn't been just taking her clothes off; he was doing it in company, with his face full of that dirty joke of his. The simplest explanation, of course, was that he knew something about her and she didn't dare take the car away or even try to collect for it. But when I'd tried a little pressure politics myself I got smeared in nothing flat. Why? I gave up, but I couldn't get rid of her entirely because random parts of her kept poking into my mind, the odd gravity about her eyes, the way she walked, and the way the top of her head reminded you of a kid with sun-burned hair. She added up to something I couldn't quite place, and then I knew what it was—an ad-writer's picture of The Girl Back Home. For God's sake, I thought. I got up and pushed some change across the counter and went out. I had to go to the bank.

I still had about two hundred dollars in a bank in Houston which I hadn't had time to get when I left there, and if I didn't put through a draft for it right away I'd be going hungry. I had about forty dollars in my pocket. I went up the street in the white sunlight, not meeting anybody and absently watching the confusion down at the other end. A shower of sparks went pin-wheeling upwards in the smoke and I decided the roof of the place must have fallen in at last.

The bank was a little deadfall on the corner, and when I went inside it was dim and a little cooler than the street. It had a couple of tellers' cages and a desk behind a railing in the rear, but there was nobody in the place—nobody at all. I stood there for a moment looking around, wondering if they operated the place like a serve-yourself market. I went over and looked through the grilles above the cages, thinking somebody might have passed out with a heart attack and be lying on the floor. Money was lying around on the shelf but there was no one in either cage.

Then I heard someone step inside the door behind me. A voice said, "Wheah the fiah, Mister Julian? Heered the sireen and the people a-runnin' but ain't nobody tell me wheah the fiah is at."

I looked around. It was a gaunt, six-foot figure, a Negro, dressed in what looked like the trousers of some kind of lodge uniform and a white T-shirt with a big, frayed straw hat on his head. Then I saw the cane and dark glasses. He was blind.

"I don't think there's anybody here, Dad," I said.

"Mister Julian must be heah. He always heah."

"Well, damned if I see him."

"You know wheah the fiah is at?" he asked.

"Yeah. Down the street just this side of the gin. It's a hamburger shack."

"Oh. Thank you, Cap'n." He turned and tapped his way out with the cane.

Just then a door in the rear opened and a man came out, apparently from a washroom. He must have been around sixty and looked like a high-school maths teacher with his vague blue eyes and high forehead with thin white hair.

He smiled apologetically. "I hope I didn't keep you waiting. Everybody's gone to the fire."

"No," I said absently. "No. Not at all."

He came over and went into one of the cages, and said something.

"What?" I hadn't been paying attention.

"I said what can I do for you?"

"Oh. I want to open an account."

I made out the draft and deposited it and went on back to the lot, still thinking about it. Everybody in this town must be fire crazy.

I sold a car that afternoon and felt a little better for a

while. I saw Gloria Harper only once, when she came out of the loan office at five o'clock with another girl. She went up the street without looking towards where I was leaning against a car on the lot. We locked up the office a little later and I got in my own car and drove over to the rooming house. It was sultry and oppressive, and after I took a shower and tried to dry myself the fresh underwear kept sticking to my perspiration-wet body. I sat in the room in my shorts and looked out the window at the back yard as the sun went down. It had a high board fence around it, a little grass turning brown with the heat, and a chinaberry tree with a dirty rabbit hutch leaning against it. This is the way it looks at thirty, I thought; anybody want to stay for forty?

After a while I put on white slacks and a shirt and went down to the restaurant. When I had eaten it was still only seven o'clock, and there was nothing except the drugstore or the movie. I wandered up that way, but it was a Roy Rogers western, so I got in the car and drove around without any thought in mind except staying out of that room as long as I could. Without knowing why, I found myself following the route we'd taken that morning, going over the sandhill past the abandoned farms and down into the bottom.

There was a slice of moon low in the west and when I parked off the road at the end of the bridge the river was a silvery gleam between twin walls of blackness under the trees. I stripped off my clothes and walked down to the sandbar and waded in. The water was a little cooler than the air and went around in a big lazy eddy in the darkness under the bridge. I circled back up the other side and waded out after a while to lie on the sandbar and look up at the stars.

I was still sweltering when I went back to the room. I couldn't sleep. In the next room an old man was reading aloud to his wife from the Bible, labouring slowly through the Book of Genesis, a begat at a time, and pronouncing it with the accent on the first syllable. I lay there on the hard slab of a bed in the heat and wondered when I'd start walking up the walls. Gloria Harper and Sutton kept going around and around in my mind, and a long time afterwards, just before I dropped off, I came back to that other thing I couldn't entirely forget. It was that bank with nobody in it.

3

THE NEXT MORNING there was another argument with
Harshaw. Just after we opened the office he wanted me to
take a cloth and dust off the cars. I was feeling low anyway
and told him the hell with it. The other salesman, an older,
sallow-faced man named Gulick, got some dust cloths out
of a desk drawer and went on out.

Harshaw leaned back in his chair and stared at me.
"What's the matter with you, Madox? You got a grudge
against the world?"

"No," I said. "I'm a salesman. When I want a job cleaning cars I'll get one."

"The way you're going, you may get one sooner than you
think. How old are you?"

"Thirty. Why?"

"Well, you haven't set the world on fire so far or you
wouldn't be here in this place."

"I wouldn't argue with you."

"You can't sell dirty cars," he grunted. "You want Gulick
to do all the work keeping 'em clean while you skim off the
gravy?"

"I'll take down my hair," I said, "and we'll both cry." I
got off the desk and went outside, disgusted with the argument and with everything. I leaned against a car, smoking a
cigarette and watching Gulick work, and after a while I
threw the butt savagely out into the street and went over
and picked up one of the cloths.

"You don't have to do this," he said, when I started in on
the other side of the car he was working on. "I don't mind
it. I like to keep busy."

He had sad brown eyes, a little like a hound's, and his

health wasn't good. The doctors had told him to work outside and he'd have to give up a job as book-keeper.

"How long have you worked for Harshaw?" I asked.

He stopped rubbing for a minute and thought about it.
He did everything very slowly and deliberately. "About a
year, I reckon."

"Hard guy to get along with, isn't he?"

"No-o. I wouldn't say that. He's just got troubles, same as
anybody."

"Troubles?"

"Got ulcers pretty bad. And then he's had a lot of family
trouble. Lost his wife a year or so ago, and he's got a boy
that——. Well, I guess you'd say he's just not much good."

"That's too bad."

"Yeah." He straightened and stretched his back. "I
always figure there's a lot of things can make a man
grouchy. He may have troubles you don't even know anything about——." He acted as if he intended to say more,
and then thought better of it and went back to work.

Harshaw came out of the office a little later and got in
one of the cars. "Going out in the country for a while," he
said to Gulick. "Be back around noon."

It was Friday and there wasn't much activity along the
street. The sun began to get hot. We had only two cars left
to dust off when I saw a young Negro in peg-top pants and
yellow shoes wander on to the end of the lot and begin
circling around an old convertible with a lot of gingerbread
on it. He kicked the tyres and backed off to look at it.

I nodded to Gulick. "Go ahead," I said. "I'll finish it."

I watched then as I rubbed off the last car. The Negro
tried the big air-horn mounted on a fender, and then they
both stood there with their hands in their pockets saying
nothing at all. Just them a blue Oldsmobile sedan slid in off
the street and stopped in front of the office. There was a
woman in it, alone. She tapped the horn.

I walked over. "Good morning. Could I help you?"

The baby-blue eyes regarded me curiously. "Oh, hello,"
she said. "I was just looking for George."

"George?"

"Mr. Harshaw," she explained. And then she added. "I'm his wife."

"Oh." It took a second for that to soak in. Gulick hadn't said Harshaw had married again. "He said he was going out in the country. I think he'll be back around noon." She must be a lot younger, I thought; she couldn't be over thirty. Somehow she made you think of an overloaded peach tree. She wasn't a big woman, and she wasn't fat, but there was no wasted space inside the seersucker suit she had on, especially around the hips and the top of the jacket. Her hair was poodle-cut and ash blonde, and her face had the same luscious and slightly over-ripe aspect as the rest of her. Maybe it was the full lower lip, and the dimples.

"Well, thanks anyway," she said. Then she smiled. "You must be the new salesman. Mr.—uh——"

"Madox," I said. "Harry Madox."

"Oh, yes. George told me about you. Well, I won't keep you from your work." She switched on the ignition and pressed the starter button. The motor didn't take hold the first time and she kept grinding at it. I'd started away, but turned now and came back.

"What do you suppose is the matter?" she asked petulantly.

"I think it's flooded. Hold the accelerator all the way to the floor while you crank it."

"Oh," she said. "Like this?"

I looked in the car. It was stupid, actually, because anybody would know how to press down on the gas to cut out an automatic choke, but I looked anyway. She had very small feet in white shoes which were mostly heels, and around one ankle, under the nylon, she had one of those gold chains women wore a year or so ago. The seersucker skirt was up over her knees. Well, I thought, she asked me to. What did she expect?

"Yes," I said. "Like that."

She jabbed at the starter again and in a moment the motor caught and took off. She smiled. "Well. How did you know that?"

"It's just one of those things you pick up."

20

"Oh. I see. Well, thanks a lot." She waved a hand and drove off.

In about twenty minutes she was back. I was sitting in the office, and when she tapped the horn I went out. "George hasn't got back yet?" she asked.

"Not yet."

"Oh, darn. He never remembers anything."

"Is there anything I can do?"

She hesitated. "I hate to ask you. I mean, you're working."

"I'm not hurting myself. What is it?"

"Well, if you *really* wouldn't mind. It'd only take a few minutes." She gestured towards the rear of the car. "I've got a lot of papers and old clothes I want to unload in our storeroom, and I promised to take the key back before noon."

"Sure," I said, "where is it?"

"Are you sure it'll be all right to leave for a few minutes?"

"Yes. Gulick can hold it down." I looked up the lot. He and the Negro boy were still rooted in the same spot, staring at the old convertible. It's like a horse trade, I thought; it'll be hours before either of them makes a move.

I slid in beside her and we started down Main Street. "It's awful nice of you," she said. "The stuff is tied up in heavy packages, and I couldn't carry it by myself."

"What is it?" I asked. "A junk drive?"

"Uh-uh. It's our club project. We store the stuff in Mr. Taylor's old building and every two or three months a junk man comes and buys the paper. We sort out the clothes and send bundles."

That's nice, I thought. They send bundles. Well, maybe it keeps them off the streets. We went down a block beyond the bank and turned right into a cross street which was only a couple of blocks long. There wasn't much here after you got off the main drag. A small chain grocery stood on the corner, and beyond that there was a Negro juke joint covered with Coca-Cola signs. She went on up to the second block and stopped in front of a building on the right. It was a boxlike two-storey frame with glass show-windows in front and vacant lots full of dead brown weeds on both sides. You could still see the lettering "TAYLOR HARDWARE" on the windows, but they were fly-specked and dirty and the place was vacant, and the door was closed with a big pad-lock. A "FOR RENT" sign leaned against the glass down in one corner. We got out and she fished around in her bag for the key. Standing up, she wasn't as tall as the Harper girl and had none of her long-legged, easy grace, but she was stacked smoothly and twelve to the dozen against the contoured retaining-wall of her clothes.

She went around and opened the trunk of the car. "I expect it'll take two trips," she said.

I glanced in. There were two bundles of old newspapers and magazines tied up with cord, and a lot of loose clothes. I hefted the papers. They weren't over fifty or seventy-five pounds each, so I gathered them up and asked her to stuff the old clothes under my arms.

She looked up at me with a kittenish smile. "Well, good-ness, I expect to carry something myself. I don't look that puny, do I?"

Let it lie, I thought. This is a small town. We went inside. The place was empty except for some old counters and shelves, and our footsteps rang with a hollow sound. There was dust everywhere. "We have to go upstairs," she said.

The stairs were in the rear. I went up first and I could hear the high heels clicking after me. All the windows were closed, and heat lay like a suffocating blanket across the lifeless air. I could feel sweat breaking out on my face. The whole second floor was a jumble of discarded junk, old pieces of furniture, loose and bundled papers, piles of cloth-ing, cast-off luggage, and even some old feather mattresses piled in a corner. A fire marshal would take one look at it, I thought, and run amok. They'd have a fire here some day that would really turn the town out. It wouldn't take much. Just some turpentine and rags . . .

"What?" I asked, suddenly aware that she had come up behind me and said something. I turned. She was throwing the clothing on a pile. Her face was flushed with the heat and there were little beads of perspiration on her upper lip.

"I said you must not know your own strength. You carried those things all the way up here, and then forgot you had them. Why don't you set them down?"

I was still holding the bundles of papers. "Oh," I said.

I threw them down. She was still looking at me, but she said nothing. It was intensely still, and hot, and there was an odd feeling of strain in the air.

"Is that all of it?" I asked.

"Yes. That's all," she said. "Thanks."

"You're welcome."

"How do you like our town?"

"All right. What I've seen of it." Why did you have to stand here and talk in this stifling hotbox up under the roof? Her face was expressionless as she watched me.

"Did you ever live in a small town?" she asked.

"Yes. I grew up in one."

"Oh? Well, you probably know what they're like, then."

"Sure."

"Well, maybe we'd better go," she said. "It's awful hot up here, don't you think?"

"It's murder." I nodded for her to go first, and we started weaving our way through the junk, towards the stairs.

"I wondered if I was just imagining it. I usually don't mind the heat, when I keep my weight down."

That was the second time she'd thrown it out there, but we understood each other about the small town now.

"Why do you want to keep your weight down?" I asked.

"She looked around at me. "Don't you think I ought to?"

"It looks perfect to me."

"Thank you."

"Not at all. It was a pleasure."

"I mean for carrying the stuff up, when Mr. Harshaw forgot."

Well, the hell with you, I thought. You just remember you're married and I won't have any trouble with you. "That's what I meant," I said. "It was a pleasure."

We went down the stairs. Just as we hit the lower floor I heard her say, "Oh, darn it. What a mess!" I looked at her, and she held out a hand covered with dirt, staring at it disgustedly. She'd forgotten about the dust and had held on to the railing.

I took out my handkerchief. "Here," I said. "Let me."

"It's all right," she said. "I think the water's still turned on in the washroom. I'll only be a minute."

She walked on back to the end of the building and disappeared into a room walled off in one corner. I stood there looking around and waiting for her, and then before I knew it I was thinking about that boar's nest of trash and junk upstairs. The place was a natural firetrap.

I don't know why I did it; there was no idea or plan in my mind. But I reached over and wiped my hand through the dust on a step, and when I saw her come out of the washroom I started back that way. "I got some of it, too," I said, holding out the hand.

There was a window in the washroom, all right, as I'd thought there would be. It was closed and locked with an ordinary latch on top of the lower sash. Before I washed my hands I reached over and took hold of the latch and unlocked it.

4

Why not? In this world you took what you wanted; you didn't stand around and wait for somebody to bring it to you. I sat on the side of the bed stark naked in the sweltering night, listening to Umlaut beget Frammis in an age-cracked voice on the other side of the wall, and thought how easy it would be. There'd be ten or fifteen thousand dollars or maybe more lying around in that comic-opera bank for a man with nerve enough to pick it up. And you could get away from the rat-race for a long time with that kind of money, with a brown-eyed girl on the beach somewhere in the Caribbean, sailing a catboat and going fishing off the reefs and drinking Cuba Libres where it's always afternoon.

Why kid myself? I wasn't a salesman. And I couldn't go back to sea, if I wanted to. I wasn't getting any younger, and another whole year was down the drain. I'd quit two jobs and got fired from three, and I'd had to get out of Houston in a hurry after a brawl with a longshoreman over some turning-basin chippy. We tore up a lot of the fixtures in a cheap beer joint by the time the thing became general, and somewhere in the confusion the longshoreman had his jaw broken with a bottle of Bacardi rum. It wasn't just an isolated incident, either; life was just a succession of jams over floozies of one kind or another.

It had been a little over a year now since the night I'd got back to the States after eleven months of that monotonous tanker shuttle between the Persian Gulf and Japan, with a four-hundred-a-month allotment to Jerilee, to find she'd shoved off with the bank account and some boy friend she'd forgotten to tell me about. I tore my second mate's

ticket into strips and flushed it down the can in a Port
Arthur ginmill and for a while I seemed to have some
purpose in life, but after I'd had time to think it over a little
I quit looking for them and threw away the gun. It wasn't
worth it. She was just another bum in a succession of them,
the only difference being that I'd been married to her.

On the other side of the wall they were piping Noah over
the rail and getting ready for the rain. Sweat ran down my
face and I thought about the bank to keep from thinking of
that Harshaw woman. Keep her weight down! She could
quit leaning it against me. But what about the bank?

It wasn't so simple, if you stopped to think about it.
When you break the law you can forget about playing the
averages because you have to win all the time. Who ever
won all the time? Yeah, but the thing which always trips
'em is association with other criminals, and I don't know
any, talkative or otherwise. An amateur's got a better
chance than the pro because nobody knows him and he
hasn't got any clippings in the files. I lay there for hours,
thinking about it.

The next day was Saturday. Harshaw was across the
street at his desk in the loan office all morning and at noon
when they closed it, he came over and said he was going
fishing for three days down at Aransas Pass.

"I'll be back on Monday night," he told Gulick. "If you
run into any snag making out papers for sale, you can
always get hold of Miss Harper."

We didn't sell anything. The town was jammed with the
usual Saturday-afternoon crowd, but nobody was looking
for a car. I prowled morosely around the lot and wondered
what Gloria Harper did when she wasn't working. Just
before we closed, the telephone rang. I answered it.

"Mr. Madox?"

I recognized the voice. So she didn't go with him, I
thought. "Yes. Madox speaking."

"This is Mrs. Harshaw. I know you'll think I'm an awful
pest, but I wonder if I could ask another favour?"

"Sure. What is it?"

"Mr. Harshaw has gone fishing, and he promised me a car off the lot while he was gone with ours, but he forgot to bring it home. I wonder if you'd drive it out for me when you close up?"

"Sure. How do I get there?"

"Go down Main Street to the bank and turn right. It's about three or four blocks beyond the edge of town. There are a couple of cross streets, I think, and then a filling station on the left. The next block is big oak trees on both sides of the street, and only two houses. Ours is the two-storey one on the right-hand side."

"Check," I said. "Which car is it?"

"He said there was a Buick. A coupé."

"Yes. It's still here. I'll bring it out."

"There's no hurry. Any time after you close up. And thanks a lot."

It was around six when we locked up the cars and the shack. I told Gulick where I was taking the coupé, and left my own car on the lot. The place wasn't hard to find, after I'd threaded my way through the double-parked congestion of Saturday-afternoon Main Street. Beyond the filling station she had spoken of, the road swung a little to the right as it entered the oaks. The house itself was back in the trees and had a big lawn in front and a gravel driveway running back beside a hedge of oleanders. It was a smaller copy of the old-style southern plantation house, with a columned porch running across the front and down one side next to the drive. I stopped by the side porch and got out. It was secluded back in here, partly cut off as it was from the street, with long shadows slanting across the lawn.

"Hello," she said.

I glanced around, but didn't see her until she opened the screen door and came out on to the porch. She had on a little-girl sort of summer dress with puffed-out short sleeves tied with bows, and was rattling ice cubes in a highball glass. She was bare-legged and wearing wedgies with grass straps, and her toenails were painted a flaming red. I don't know anything about women's clothes, but still I was conscious that she jarred somehow. The teenage dress didn't do anything for that over-ripe figure except to wander on to the track and get run over, and she looked like a burlesque queen in bobby socks.

"Oh, hello," I said. "I left the keys in it."

"Thanks. It was sweet of you to drive it out for me."

"Not at all."

"How about a drink before you go?"

"Yeah. Sure."

I followed her inside. The venetian blinds were half closed in the living room and a big electric fan oscillated like a slowly shaking head on the mantel above the fireplace. She stopped and faced me, and again I could feel that faint strain in the air.

"Bourbon and water?"

"That's fine."

"Push some of those magazines out of the way and sit down. I'm sorry the place's in such a mess." She turned to go, and then stopped and added, as if it was an afterthought, "I gave the girl the week-end off, to visit her folks."

She went out. It was hot in the room, even with the fan going, and I was conscious of a deep quiet, unbroken except by the whirring of the fan blades and now and then a tinkle of ice against glass out in the kitchen. I lighted a cigarette and put the match in a tray. It was heaped up and overflowing with butts smeared with lipstick. Movie and confession magazines were scattered over the sofa and lying on the floor, and I could see the rings left by highball glasses on the coffee table. Standing there looking around at the evidence of boredom was like watching a burning fuse.

She came back in a minute with the drink, and I saw she'd refilled her own. She sat down in the big chair across from me with her legs stretched out and the toes of the wedgies touching each other, and looked at me with her chin propped on her hand.

"Well, how are you standing the excitement?"

I shrugged. "Maybe it picks up on Saturday night."

"Yes, it really does. They show two westerns at the movie instead of one."

"Sounds pretty rugged."

"Well, you can always join the Ladies' Club and collect junk. There's a hot pastime."

"I might have trouble getting past the credentials committee."

"I bet you wouldn't if you approached 'em one at a time. Meow."

"What a way to talk about the Ladies!"

"They're a bunch of dears."

I put my glass on the coffee table and walked over to the front window to look out through the venetian blind. The house across the street was a little further up and you couldn't see it from here.

"Which one of 'em lives over there?" I asked.

"Mrs. Gross. She's the one with fourteen eyes and party-line ears."

She put her glass down and walked over and stood close to me. "Well, what do you think of the view?"

I turned, and we were staring at each other again. "It's better all the time."

"Oh, I meant to ask you. Did you have any trouble finding the place?"

"No," I said. "I could find it in the dark."

"Are you sure?" she asked.

I put a hand behind her neck and then brought it up in back of the ash-blonde curls, holding it there and pulling her face against mine, hard, as I kissed her. Her mouth was soft and moist, and she came to me like a dachshund jumping into your lap. In a minute she turned her face aside and pushed back.

"You'd better get out."

"Like hell."

"I thought you told me you'd lived in a small town."

"What of it?"

"Don't you think that old witch over there watched you drive in here? And she's watching right now, waiting for you to leave."

I tried to take hold of her again, but she moved back, pushing at my arms. "Harry, get out!"

I could see she meant it, and somehow I had sense enough to realize she was right. There was no use asking for trouble.

"All right," I said. "But don't think you can tease me. I'll be back."

She didn't say anything.

"Well?"

Her face was sullen. "Well?" she said.

I picked up my car at the lot and drove over to the rooming house. After standing under the shower a long time, I changed into slacks and T-shirt and drove down to Main. It was dusk now, with heat lying motionless and sticky in the streets, and bugs danced through the beams of weaving headlights. It was hard finding a parking place, but I finally beat two other cars to one in front of the bank and sat there for a while trying to push the sultry weights of Dolores Harshaw off my mind. She was dangerous in a town like this. The hell with her; I wouldn't go back. But wouldn't I? What about later on? Keeping the thought of her out of that bleak hotbox of a room was going to be like trying to dam a river with a tennis racket.

I shook my head irritably, and stared at the bank. A light was burning over the vault in the rear, and I could see the layout of the whole room through the glass doors in front of me. The over-all depth would be about fifty feet, and the side door which came in off the cross street was well back, not over twenty feet this side of the vault and the door which probably led into a washroom or closet of some kind. I turned my head and tried to picture about where the old Taylor building would be from here. Down one block, I thought, and two to the right, which would put it diagonally in front of the bank. That was about right. *About right for what?* I cursed and threw away the cigarette I was smoking and got out to stand on the sidewalk.

I was too restless and irritable to think of eating, so I started walking aimlessly up the sidewalk through the crowd. Up in the next block I went past the drugstore and as I glanced in through the window I saw Gloria Harper in front of the magazine racks. Without stopping to wonder why, I opened the screen door and went in.

She was still absorbed in the magazines and didn't see me.

"Hello," I said.

She glanced up abruptly. "Oh, hello, Mr. Madox." She didn't smile, but there was nothing unfriendly in the way she looked at me.

"How about a soda?"

She considered it thoughtfully. "Why, yes. Thank you."

She paid the clerk for the magazine and we went back to one of the booths across from the fountain.

"First," I said, "I'm sorry about the other day. I must have had the book open at the wrong place."

The violet eyes glanced up at me, and then became confused and looked away. "It's all right," she said.

"Then you're not mad at me?"

She shook her head. "Not any more."

"That's fine," I said. "Now we can start even again. Next time I'll read the instructions on the bottle. What do you do around here on Saturday nights?"

"Not much. There's just the movie. And sometimes a dance, but not this week."

"How about going swimming, then?"

"I'd like to, but I couldn't tonight. I'm baby-sitting."

"You must be a big operator, with two jobs. What're you trying to do, get rich?"

"No, it's just in the family. I'm staying with my sister's little girl so she and her husband can go to the movies."

"Oh. Well, I'll drive you out there."

"It's only five or six blocks."

"I'll drive you anyway."

She smiled. "Well, all right. Thank you."

I watched her while she finished the soda, thinking of that odd gravity about everything she did, and the way she always said "Thank you," instead of just "Thanks." A sweet kid from a nice family, you'd say; probably teaches a Sunday-school class and goes steady with some guy in his last year at law school. The only hitch was—where did Sutton fit in? How about the way he'd looked at her, with that secret and very dirty joke of his? It was impossible, and still there it was.

She told me how to get there and we drove out Main, going north past the used-car lot. I asked her a little about herself, and she told me she'd lived around here most of her life except for a couple of years away at school. Her mother and father had moved to California and she was living with her sister and brother-in-law. I slipped over a couple of oblique questions, looking for a steady boy friend, but she let them slide off without saying one way or the other. She didn't wear any engagement ring, though. I looked.

It was a small white house on a gravelled side street, complete with a white picket fence and a young tree in the yard. "Won't you come in?" she asked.

Why not? "Sure," I said. "Thanks."

There were no street lights, but the moon was waxing, and higher now, and I could see the dark shadow of vines growing along the fence and over the porch. The air was heavy and sweet with something I hadn't smelled for a long time, and after the second breath I knew it was honeysuckle. To make it perfect, I thought, the gate should drag a little and need to be listed to open it. It did.

All the lights were off and they were sitting on the porch steps. When they saw there was somebody with her, they reached inside the front door and turned on the porch light. The sister was a slightly older version of Gloria, a little heavier, maybe, and having grey eyes instead of the startling violet. They were friendly, but a little embarrassed, like people who didn't get around very much. Gloria introduced me. His name was Robinson, and he was a slightly built man around my age with thinning yellow hair and rimless glasses.

"Mr. Madox is the new salesman at the lot," Gloria said.

"And apprentice baby-sitter," I added, clowning a little to break the ice. We shook hands.

"Well, you don't look as if they could overpower you," he said, and grinned.

As they went out the gate Mrs. Robinson called back, "Make Mr. Madox some lemonade, Gloria."

"Thanks," I said. "We just had a soda."

I didn't notice the child until they had gone. She was maybe two or four years old or something like that, curled up in a long nightgown in the porch swing, a golden-haired girl with big saucer eyes. The whole place, I thought, is as blonde as an old-country smörgäsbord.

"This is Gloria Two," she said. "And this gentleman is Mr. Madox, honey-lamb."

I never know what to say to kids. That itchy-kitchy-coo stuff makes me as sick as it probably makes them, so I just said, "How do you do?" Surprisingly, she stared back at me as gravely as her aunt and said, "How do you do?"

Then I thought of the funny name. "Gloria Two?" I asked.

Gloria Harper smiled. "They named her after me. And then when I came to live here it was a little confusing. Mostly we just call her 'Honey.'"

"Isn't that confusing too?" I asked.

She stopped smiling. "Why?"

"Doesn't anybody call you that?"

"No."

"They should. It's the colour of your hair."

She shook her head. "It's just sunburned."

She took Gloria Two inside to put her to bed. When she came back I was admiring the water colours on the walls in the living room. I recognized one of them as being the wooden bridge over the river, the one we'd crossed going out to the oil well.

"They're good," I said. "Did you do them?"

She nodded. "I don't have much talent, but it's fun."

"I like them."

"Thank you," she said.

We went out and sat down on the porch with our feet on the steps. A cocker spaniel came around the corner, looked me over, and jumped into the porch swing. I handed Gloria charles williams

a cigarette and we smoked, not saying much. The honeysuckle vines looked like patent leather in the moonlight and
the night was heavy with their perfume.

"It's pretty, isn't it?" she asked quietly. "Sometimes when
it's quiet like this you can hear the whip-poor-wills."

We listened for them and it was very still now, but we
didn't hear any.

"Well," she said. "They're kind of sad anyway."

"They're an echo or something. I think the ones you hear
have been dead for a thousand years or so."

She turned her head and looked at me. "Yes. I never
thought of it before, but that's the way they are."

Her eyes were large, and they looked black here in the
shadows. "You're very pretty," I said.

"Thank you. But it's just the moonlight."

"No," I said. "I wasn't talking about the lighting."

She didn't say anything. I snapped the cigarette and it
sailed across the fence. "Look," I said. "What's with
Sutton?"

You could see her tighten up. She was there, and then
she was going away. "I don't know what you mean."

"Well, I guess it *isn't* any of my business."

"Please——" Her voice was strung out tight and she was
unhappy and scared of something. "It's—— You're just
imagining things, Mr. Madox."

I started to say something, but just then a car pulled up
in front of the gate and stopped. A boy in white slacks got
out and came up the walk. He was about twenty-one and
his name was Eddie Something and he was home from
school for the summer. The three of us sat on the steps and
talked for a while, about how hot it was and about school
and about how many of them were going right into the
Army.

"What outfit were you in, Mr. Madox?" Eddie Something
asked.

"Navy. I got out on a medical and went into the
merchant marines." I thought of the "Mr. Madox" and the
fact that we were talking about two armies ten years apart.
What was I doing here, talking to these kids? Getting off

34

the steps, I flipped the cigarette away and said, "Well, I'll see you around."

"You don't have to go, do you?" Gloria asked.

"Yeah," I said. I went out and got in the car and rammed it towards the highway, full of a black restlessness and angry at everything. Driving around didn't do any good. I drove out to the river and went swimming, and when I came back to town it was still only ten o'clock. The rooming house was thunderously silent. Even the old couple in the next room had gone somewhere. I mopped the sweat off my face and tried to sit still on the bed.

Well? she said. She sat on the chair with her legs stretched out and the toes of the wedgies touching and stared at me, sulky-eyed, over ripe, and spoiling, and said, *Well?*

Well?

Everything was distorted perhaps because of the moonlight. Shadows were swollen and dead black and nothing looked the same as it did in the day. The filling station was a hot oasis of light, but I was behind it, walking fast along the alley. Beyond it I crossed the road and went into the trees. I pushed through the oleander hedge and stood for a moment in its shadow, looking at the house and the lawn. The only car in the drive was the Buick coupé, right where I'd left it, and all the windows in the house were dark. I went up the porch.

The screen door was unlatched.

A little light came in through the venetian blinds in the living room. There was no one in it. I located the stairs and went up. The short hallway at the top had two doors in it and a window at the end. One of the doors was open.

She was lying on the bed next to a window looking out over the back yard. From the waist up she was in deep shadow, but moonlight slanted in across the bottom of the bed and I could see the gleam of that tiny chain around her ankle.

"Harry," she said, her voice a little thick with the whisky. "You found the way, didn't you?"

What's so wonderful about it? I thought. Dogs do.

5

"HARRY?"

"What?"

"You want another drink?"

"No."

"Why not?"

"I've had enough. I've got a headache."

"It couldn't be the whisky. It's straight Bourbon. It wouldn't give you a headache."

Nothing but the best, I thought. "All right. It's not the whisky."

"I like you," she said. "You don't drink much, but you're all right. Harry, you know what?"

"What?"

"You're all right."

"You said that."

"Well, Godsakes, I'll say it again if I want to. You're all right. You're sweet. You're a big ugly bastard with a face that'd stop a clock, but you're sweet. You know what I mean?"

"No." I lighted a cigarette and lay on my back staring up at the ceiling. It must be nearly midnight. My head throbbed painfully and very slowly, like a big flywheel turning over, and the taste of whisky was sour in my mouth. She must bathe in cologne, I thought; the room was drenched with it.

"Harry?"

"What is it?"

"You don't think I'm fat, do you?"

"Of course not."

"You wouldn't kid 'ninnocent young girl, would you?"

"No." I turned and looked at her. Moonlight from the window had moved up the bed and now it fell diagonally across her from the waist up to the big spread-out breast which rocked a little as she shook the ice in her glass. I thought of a full and slightly bruised peach beginning to spoil a little. She was somewhere between luscious and full-bloom and in another year or so of getting all her exercise lying down and lifting the bottle she'd probably be blowzy.

"Well?" she said sarcastically. "Maybe I ought to turn on the light."

"You asked me a question. Did you want it answered or didn't you?"

She giggled. "Oh, don't be so touchy. I was just kidding you. I don't mind. Pour me another drink."

She didn't need any more, but I reached down beside the bed for the bottle. Anything to get her to shut up, I thought. The bottle was empty.

"There's not any more," I said.

"The hell there's not. What became of it?"

"Maybe it leaks," I said wearily.

"Nuts. We got to have a drink." She sat up in bed and climbed out unsteadily, whisky-and-cologne smelling and sexy, bosom aswing, and humming "You'd Be So Easy To Love," under her breath. "I got some more hid in the kitchen. Have to keep it hid from him because he don't drink and won't let me, when he's home. Him and his lousy ulcers."

I heard her bump into something in the living room and swear. She had a bos'n's vocabulary. My head felt worse and I wondered why I didn't get out of there. She was already on the edge of being sloppy drunk, kittenish one minute and belligerent the next. God knows I've always had some sort of affinity for gamey babes, but she was beginning to be a little rough even for me. She had a lot of talent, but it was highly specialized and when you began to get up to date in that field you were wasting your time just hanging around for the conversation. You could do without it.

In a few minutes she came back carrying what looked

like a tray of ice cubes and another bottle of whisky. She set the ice cubes on the dresser and I could see her fumbling around on the top of it for something.

"Harry, we're going to have a drink," she said thickly. "Good old Harry ... Harry is a girl's best friend.... Oh, where'd I put those dam' cigarettes? Harry, switch on that light, will you? I got to have a smoke."

I reached up and turned on the reading lamp. She found what she was looking for and turned around, the cigarette hanging out of her mouth and that gold chain around her ankle, looking at me with a lazy, half-drunken smile.

"Harry, you don't think I'm fat, do you?"

Here we go again, I thought. "No," I said.

She smiled again. "Well, you sure ought to know." She had the bottle of whisky in her hands and was trying to twist the cap off. She paused for a moment, apparently thinking hard about something, and laughed. "Say, you really had a nerve, didn't you?"

"Why?"

"Coming into the house the way you did. And right into my room."

Maybe it *was* risky, I thought. I might have got caught in the traffic.

"What would you of done if I'd screamed?"

"I don't know," I said. "Run, I suppose."

"But you didn't think I would, did you?"

"I didn't know."

"But you was pretty sure of it, wasn't you?" There was a little edge to her voice.

"I told you I didn't know."

"The hell you didn't." She quit working on the bottle and glared at me. "I know what you thought. And you know what?"

"What?"

"I don't give a damn. What do you know about that?"

"Oh, knock it off," I said.

"I know what you think, all right."

"You said that."

"Think I'm some lousy tramp that you can walk right

into her room, will you? Well, I'll tell you what you can
do——"

"You're drunk," I said. "Why don't you shut up?"

"Shut up, will I? Why don't you make me?"

"Who hasn't?" I said.

The bottle slid out of her hands. She picked up the tray
of ice cubes and let fly. It bounced off my ribs and ice slid
all over me. I got off the bed and started for her. She was a
sight, arm drawn back and bristling with drunken rage and
as nude as a calendar girl. I grabbed her arm and swung
her, and she shot backwards and fell across the bed. All the
fight went out of her and she crumpled and began to cry.

"Harry," she sobbed, turning on her back and looking up
at me with her eyes swimming." Where you going, Harry?"

"Nuts," I said.

The moon was almost down now, and the streets were
deserted and dark with shadow. Two blocks away on Main
a car went past now and then, but here beside the old
Taylor building there was no light or movement. I stopped
and stared at it, trying to fight off the disgust and the
headache and escape the cloying perfume.

Across the weed-filled vacant lot on this side, next to the
cross street, I could just make out the small window at the
rear, the one I had unlocked. It might be weeks or months
before anybody discovered it and fastened the latch. I had
plenty of time to make up my mind about it, but what was I
waiting for? Didn't I know what was going to happen as
surely as sunrise if I went on living in the same town with
that sexy lush?

Oh, sure, I'd stay away from her, all right. Didn't I
always? What was my batting average so far in staying out
of trouble when it was baited with that much tramp? It was
an even zero, and I didn't see anything in the situation here
that promised I'd improve very much. And the way she
soaked up the booze, and as crazy as she was when she was
drunk, she was about as safe to be mixed up with in a town
like this as a rattlesnake. You didn't know what she'd
do.

The smart thing was to get out of here and let her happen to somebody else.

But I had to wait, unless I wanted to give up the idea which was going around in my mind. It would take at least a month. No, it would take longer, because you couldn't just come in here, pull off something like that, and then run. It would put the finger on you. I looked at the building again. It was perfect for what I wanted—unoccupied, and not too near any of the few inhabited shacks along the street. The only hitch was that I had to get into it and out again without being seen, when the time came, and now the moon was working against me. I couldn't take a chance on it until it started to wane, unless we happened to get an overcast or a rainy night. There were two or three shacks on the opposite side of the cross street which had a view of the side of the building, and you could never tell when somebody might be awake and looking out from one of them.

I went on back to the rooming house and lay awake a long time still thinking about it. Sometime before I dropped off I got to wondering what was on that street next to the bank, the one the side door opened on to. I had been right there on the corner a couple of times, but I couldn't remember. If there were a store on the opposite side with a door or show windows facing the side of the bank it would be too dangerous. That was something I had to find out before I could even consider it, but it could wait until morning.

The next day was Sunday. I awoke around ten with a hang-over and feeling as if I'd been beaten up in a fight, listless and only half alive. I went downtown for some orange juice and coffee, bought a paper at the drugstore, and then walked slowly around the whole block the bank was on.

It was all right. In fact, it was very good. The cross street was blind as far as seeing the side door of the bank was concerned. There was a store across there, all right, but it faced only on Main and this side was a blank brick wall. I went on around, as if out for an aimless Sunday morning

stroll. Directly behind the bank there was an alley cutting
all the way through the block, and where it came out into
the next street the only business establishments again faced
on Main. All right, I thought; so far, so good.

Tuesday, when the draft had gone through, I went back
to the bank and cashed a cheque for fifty dollars. While I
was inside I looked it over again, very thoroughly. There
were four men at work, one in each of the two cages, an
officer of some kind at the railed-in desk, and a book-keeper
busy over the tabulating machines. They were all young or
in early middle age except the Mr. Chips type I'd talked to
before. He would be the one who'd always get left there
because he was too old and frail to belong to the volunteer
fire department. The door at the rear was partly open this
time and I could see it led into a washroom, all right. And
it opened inward.

I was beginning to get it all into place in my mind now.
The tough part was going to be the waiting. Right now I
had to work out the idea for the machine, and I already
had a pretty good idea about that. I had to go out of town
to buy the things I needed, however. It would be too risky
to do it around here, or keep it in my room while I was
working on it. You lived in a glass bowl in a town this
small. On Thursday I told Harshaw I was going to take the
next day off to drive down to Houston and try to collect
some money a man owed me.

I hadn't seen any more of Dolores Harshaw at all, but
Thursday afternoon I ran into Gloria Harper in the drug
store. I had gone in for a Coke at three o'clock and she was
sitting alone in a booth. She looked up and smiled, and I
went over and sat down.

"Are you doing anything tonight?" I asked.

She shook her head. "Not tonight."

"Well, I hear they're playing 'The Birth of a Nation' at
the movie. Why don't we go see it?"

"It isn't really that bad, is it?" she asked. "But I'd love to
go." Her smile was something to see; and I noticed I was
beginning to look for it when I was around her.

I picked her up around seven. The picture wasn't too bad, but we ran out on the second feature. As we were walking back up the street to the car she stopped and bought a pencil from the old blind Negro, the one who had come into the bank. He had a little stand there on the sidewalk.

"How are you tonight, Uncle Mort?" she asked.

"Jes' fine, Miss Gloahia," he said. "Thank you."

He'd recognized her by her voice. "Who is he?" I asked as we went on and got in the car.

"Just Mort. He's been there in that spot fifteen hours a day six days a week since I was in rompers. Maybe he's been there forever," she said.

"Did you need a pencil?"

She blushed. "Well, you can always use one."

We drove around for a while and when I took her home the house was dark. The Robinsons were gone somewhere. We stood by the gate for a moment in the moonlight. I was conscious of thinking she wasn't merely pretty; she was one of the loveliest girls I had ever seen in my life. For a moment I was like an awkward kid; I wanted to kiss her and I was afraid to.

"Well, good night," I said.

"Good night," she said. "And thank you. I enjoyed the picture very much."

Well, if you're not a silly bastard, I thought. Why didn't you ask her to go to the church supper?

I shoved off around ten the next morning, but I didn't go to Houston. I drove over to a fair-sized town about a hundred miles away, a place I'd never been before. I got a room at a tourist court and then went shopping.

At a drugstore I picked up a hand-wound alarm clock. Then I bought two rolls of surgical cotton at another one, and went around to two or three five-and-ten-cent stores for the rest. I got a cheap soldering-iron, a little solder, a pair of pliers, a short piece of heavy copper wire, and some big sheets of oo sandpaper. I mentally checked it off the list. That was about all except some thread and a small flashlight. After I bought those I dropped into a market and bought a carton of canned beer and a box of big kitchen matches and got the clerk to give me a cardboard box about a foot wide and eighteen inches long. I went back to the motel, put the beer in the little refrigerator to keep cold, drew the blinds, and went to work on the clock.

I took the bell cover off, exposing the clapper or striker. After plugging in the soldering-iron, I cut off two pieces of the copper wire just a little shorter than the thickness of the clock from front to back. When the iron was hot enough, I soldered them side by side on top of the clapper, putting on lots of solder and making it as rigid as I could. Then I wound the clock, set the alarm, and tried it out. The wire cross-arm vibrated nicely and held together all right.

Going out to the kitchenette, I opened a can of beer and came back to look at what I'd done so far. I'd know in a few minutes whether I could depend on it or not. I took a drink of the beer, lighted a cigarette, and went on with the job. First, I wrapped a sheet of sandpaper around each of the two rolls of cotton and made it fast with some of the thread. Then I took four of the big kitchen matches, laid them together with two pointing each way and overlapping a little in the centre, and placed them on the cross-arm I'd soldered on to the bell clapper. I secured them with several turns of the thread, letting them stick out about a half inch over the clock in front and back. After winding and setting the alarm, I placed the clock upright in the bottom of the box the market clerk had given me, and put in the two sandpaper covered rolls, one on each side. It didn't fit right; the rolls were too large and tended to bind the clapper cross-arm so it couldn't move freely. It had to have just the right amount of tension; that was the reason I'd used cotton to back up the sandpaper instead of something solid. A block of wood or something like that would do if you got the spacing absolutely correct to within a sixty-fourth of an inch or so, but if you didn't the matches might not touch at all or it might be too close and bind.

I took out the rolls of cotton, pulled some of it off, and rewrapped them with the sandpaper. This time it was just right. The match heads pressed with just the right tension against the slightly yielding wall of sandpaper. Good, I thought. I took another drink of beer and sat back to wait. In a minute there was a click and the alarm went off, the cross-arm vibrating wildly. The match heads whirred against the sandpaper and all four of them burst into flame.

I tried it twelve times, and it never failed once. I took off the burnt matches for the last time and sat back with my beer to look at it. And that was when it really came home to me what I was about to do. I was going to rob a bank, committing the additional crime of arson in the process, and if I got caught I'd go to prison.

Well, I thought, go on selling second-hand jalopies for another forty years and maybe somebody'll give you a testimonial and a forty-dollar watch.

6

WHEN I GOT BACK I left the whole thing in the trunk of the car. If I took it into my room the nosy old girl who ran the place would probably be in it the first time she cleaned, and it was crazy enough to start her wondering. I already had a blanket in the car, an old one which had been in it when I bought it eight months ago. That was safe enough; nobody would ever trace it. I still had to have a piece of line, though, and I didn't want to buy it because something like that was too easy for a clerk to remember. If I kept my eyes open I should find a short length around somewhere.

I checked right in at the lot when I got to town and didn't go out to the rooming house until after work. There were two letters for me on the hall table, addressed in the same hand and postmarked here in town, but with no return address on them. I sat down on the bed and tore them open.

"Dear Harry," the first one said. "Please call me. I miss you so and I'm sorry I acted the way I did. I want to see you so bad. Your loving Friend." There was no signature. Well, at least she had that much sense.

I spread the other one open. "Harry," she had scrawled, "why don't you call me? Why? I can't stand not hearing from you. I told you I was sorry, what more can I do? I've just got to see you."

Was she crazy? I tore the letters into strips and burned them in the ash-tray, feeling a little chill of apprehension go over me. What would she do next? And the next time she got plastered?

The following day was Sunday. I drove out the highway

after I'd had breakfast and turned off on to the dirt road going towards the river bottom and the oil well. When I got up in the pine on the sandhill near the old abandoned farms I found a pair of ruts leading off into the timber where I could get the car off the road and out of sight. It was a beautiful morning, still and hot, with the heavy scent of pine in the air, and it was good to be out here alone and away from town. I got out and started walking up the hill, keeping away from the road. In a little while I found what I was looking for, the remains of an old pine on the ground, the sap wood long since rotted away and only the heart and pine knots remaining. I didn't have an axe, but it was easy to lay it across another log and break off a section of the heart by jumping on it. I looked at the end where it had broken. It was pure pitch pine, the kind we used for kindling when I was a boy.

I was about to start back to the car with it when I noticed I was near the edge of the clearing where one of the abandoned farmhouses stood. Leaving the chunk of pine in an open place where I could find it again, I circled the edge of the field and came up behind the house. The doors were torn off, and there wasn't much in it, just dust and cobwebs and pieces of glass here and there from the broken windows. I walked on through to the front door and looked out. The road was in plain sight from here, the sand blazing white in the sun, but it was completely deserted and I couldn't hear any sound of a car. The barn was off to the left of the house a short distance across the sand and dead weeds. I went over and looked in.

It was shadowy and cool, with a faint odour of dusty hay and old manure. There was a loft overhead which appeared to be empty, and a walled-off corn crib in one corner, in front of the stalls and feed-boxes. I went over and looked into the crib, and found just what I was looking for. An old horse collar with the stuffing coming out of it was hanging from a harness peg on the wall, and dangling from the same peg was a piece of discarded rope ploughline possibly ten feet long. I took it in my hands and tested it. It was very old, but plenty strong enough for what I wanted.

I was coiling it up when I stopped suddenly and listened. A car was approaching out there on the road. I could hear it plainly now, the motor lugging in the heavy sand. I shook off the sudden nervousness and swore under my breath. I was too jumpy. It was only Sutton, either going to town or just now coming home from Saturday night. But the car didn't go on past. I heard it slowing down, and then it was turning in. It stopped in front of the house.

I was sweating. It wasn't that I was doing anything wrong, but just that I'd look suspicious and attract attention, the very thing I didn't want, if somebody saw me prowling around out here. What explanation could I give for my being here in this old barn, with my car parked a half mile away in the timber? I whirled, looking for a way to get out or a place to hide. I couldn't leave by the door. That was in plain sight of the house. But two planks had been torn off the rear wall, and I might be able to squeeze out there. I started to run back to it when I noticed a small hole in the wall next to the house. Maybe I could find out who it was and what he was up to. Whoever it was might leave in a minute, anyway, without coming near the barn. I could see the house and the car pulled up in front of it. And it wasn't a man getting out of the car. It was Gloria Harper.

It threw me for a minute. What would she be doing out here? And what the devil was she unloading out of the car and putting on the porch. It looked like a fruit jar and a china plate, as nearly as I could tell, and there was something else which resembled a bread board. Was she going to set up housekeeping in that broken-down shack?

She had something in her hand now which looked like little sticks, and then I began to catch on. They were paint brushes. It was a water colour outfit she had, and the thing I'd thought was a bread board must be a block of paper. She had on a pair of brief white shorts and a striped T-shirt, and the long-legged, easy way she moved was enough to make you catch your breath.

She got all of her equipment together and sat down in

the shade on the edge of the porch with her feet on the steps and the block of paper on her legs, and began sketching the barn with long strokes of a pencil or charcoal stick. After she had it blocked in she started mixing paints in the white plate, dipping her brushes in the jar of water. She was completely absorbed in what she was doing and, alone like this and not knowing she was being watched, there was something almost radiant about her face, somehow sweet and infinitely appealing and still full of that quiet dignity she had. I wanted to go out there where she was.

Was I blowing my top? I couldn't go out there. How would I explain why I'd been hiding in the barn? But wait, I thought. She'd be here for a long time yet. I could sneak out the back of the barn and get into the timber without her seeing me, go back and get the car, and just happen to be driving by on my way to the river to go swimming. That would be plausible enough.

I had just started to turn away when somebody beat me to it. I heard a car coming along the road, and then I knew whoever it was had seen her there on the porch because he slowed abruptly and turned in. I looked back towards the house. She had put down the brush and was watching apprehensively as the man got out of his car. It was Sutton.

He walked over to the porch and said something I couldn't hear. I watched her, and it wasn't uneasiness alone that was in her expression; there was loathing too. Knowing they wouldn't be watching the barn now, I moved to the front door and peered out. I could hear them there. I waited.

"And how's my little chum today?" he said.

"If you mean me," she said, "I'm very well, thank you."

"Well, you *look* nice, honey. Nice outfit, too." He grinned and looked her up and down, taking it off as he went. "And you sure have the legs for it, haven't you, baby?"

"Did you want to see me about something?" she asked coldly.

"No. No. Just stopped for a minute to say hello. By the way, where's your friend this morning?"

"Which friend?"

"Big Boy, what's his name."

"Do you mean Mr. Madox?"

"I guess so. Anyway, the guy you came out to the house with the other day. I saw you going to the movies the other night, and figured you was kind of chummy. Maybe he's a little funny, too, huh?"

"Funny?" I could see the revulsion on her face.

"You know what I mean, baby."

I could feel my hands digging against the door frame. Was that what was behind that dirty joke of his and the contemptuous grin? He couldn't mean anything else, the way he had said it. But to her? Was he crazy? Or just stupid?

"Would you leave now?" she asked, her voice on the ragged edge of going all to pieces. "Or would you mind if I did?"

"Oh, I was just going. But you mind if I see your picture? I'm a great art lover, myself."

Without a word she tore it off the block and handed it to him, as if she didn't want him to defile more than one sheet of paper. He took it and pretended to study it with great seriousness, holding it at arm's length and nodding his head like an instructor.

"Promising," he said. "Very promising. But, honey, don't you think it needs a little red? To kind of overburden the harmisfralcher?"

She said nothing. He reached down for one of the brushes, dipped it into the plate, and smeared it across the paper. He handed it back to her. She let it slide to the ground. It was sickening.

I started out the door, and caught myself just in time. What was I, a sap? He wasn't bothering me, was he? I was supposed to be looking out for Harry Madox, not making a chump of myself for nothing. I stayed where I was.

"Well, I'll see you around, baby," he said. He got in his car and drove off.

She sat there for a few minutes after he left, just staring

off at nothing, and then she slowly gathered everything up and put it in the car. When she was out of sight down the road I walked over to the porch. The picture was lying face up in the sand. I picked it up. It looked fine except for the smear of red he had drawn across it from one corner to the other. He liked his little joke, all right.

One of these days somebody would probably kill him. I wondered who.

Monday evening while I was putting on a fresh shirt the landlady knocked on the door.

"Telephone, Mr. Madox."

I went down the hall to the phone. "Hello. Madox," I said.

"Harry," she said, "why didn't you call me?"

"You think I'm crazy?"

"I want to see you, Harry."

"Look——"

"I miss you."

I started to tell her to go to hell and then hang up, but I didn't. I began to think about her. She could do that to you, even on the phone. Maybe it was because her voice matched the rest of her.

"Where are you?" I asked.

"At the drugstore. I thought I'd go to the movie, but again I may not. I'm sort of restless—you know how it is. So I might go for a ride."

"Yes."

"Maybe up the highway about five miles to where a road turns off to the right and goes over to an old sawmill. It's not hard to find. Once you get on the road you can't get off."

I put the phone back on the cradle. She'd said it, all right. Once you got on the road you couldn't get off.

I tried to eat some dinner, but it was straw and it choked me. I walked restlessly up the sidewalk, going nowhere. Sutton was in front of the pool hall with a handful of numbers from a tip board, reading them and throwing them on the sidewalk. He nodded and we looked at each other. I thought of what he had said to Gloria Harper. He liked his laughs so well, why not shag him one in the mouth and watch him laugh his teeth out? Why not mind his own business? He wasn't shoving me around, was he? And I wasn't Gloria Harper's mother.

I got in the car. Why try to pretend I wasn't going out there? Did I think I could kid myself? I found the road without any trouble. The moon wasn't up yet, and it was very dark under the trees. The old sawmill was on the side of a wooded ravine a mile or so from the highway. I saw a dilapidated shed and a pile of sawdust in the headlights, but there was no other car. I cut the lights and sat there, waiting, but I was too restless to sit still very long and got out and walked around.

I heard the car coming then. It stopped under the trees and the lights went off. The ceiling light came on momentarily and I knew she had opened the door to get out. I walked over. I could see her very faintly, just the blur of her face and the blonde head, but she couldn't see me at all.

"Where are you?" she asked.

I didn't answer. I stepped closer and reached out and put my hands on her. She gasped, and turned, her arms reaching out, groping for me. I kissed her roughly and her arms tightened about my neck with an urgent wild strength in them. She twisted her face a little to one side and her mouth whispered against my cheek, "Harry, I just had to see you."

She was partly right, anyway. She just had to see somebody.

We were in the car with moonlight spilling into the other side of the ravine. "Do you love me, Harry?" she asked.

"No," I said.

"Well, that's a fine answer. You might at least say you did."

"Why should I?"

"I just thought it might sound better that way. It don't make any difference, though, does it?"

"No."

"I suppose you think I'm in love with you, don't you?"

"And why would I?"

"Because I'm here. Well, let me tell you——"

"You don't have to tell me. I know why you're here. But you don't think we're going to get by with much of this, do you?"

"Why not?"

"And you're the one who asked me if *I'd* lived in a small town."

"It's all right. He's at a lodge meeting."

"It's dangerous as hell. You know that."

"I notice you're telling me that now. You didn't say anything about it a couple of hours ago."

"You didn't expect me to think then, did you?"

She laughed. "How's about another kiss, and to hell with the sermon." She was a witch, all right. She leaned back against me with her head in my arms and her feet on the window, bare legs a faint gleam in the darkness.

"Why'd you marry him?" I asked.

"I don't know. Maybe I was just getting scared. I'd been married twice before and it didn't work out, and I was trying to make a living out of a crumby little beauty shop and not getting any younger. I'd known him a long time. He used to come and see me when he was in Houston. It was a kind of a—arrangement, I guess you'd call it. And then, after his wife died——" She paused for a moment, and then went on irritably. "Oh, hell, I don't know. He just kept after me about it till I gave in. How'd I know it was such a dump?"

"Well, why do you stay?" I asked.

"What're you kicking about? You seem to be doing all right." She was rugged; there was no doubt of that.

"You think you're going to get by with this forever?"

"Who the hell cares about forever? Forever's when you're dead."

Yeah, I thought; forever's when you're dead all right, but you don't have to rush it. She was as crazy as frozen dynamite. I wanted to ditch her, and I knew that as long as

I was around this town I never could, unless she got mad enough to ditch me. I'd always come back. In the only field of activity she cared anything about, she was terrific.

I didn't see her for a couple of days, and then on Thursday night I was too busy to think about her. It was the cloudy night I'd been waiting for.

7

I WENT TO THE MOVIE and sat through a double feature without seeing it, feeling the tension beginning. When I came out at 11:30 it was still overcast, with thunder growling far off in the west. I got in the car and drove a long way down the highway, beyond the river, killing time which died too slowly. It was a little after one when I came back to town, the streets deserted now and the only lights the all-night café and a filling station on the other end of Main. I circled through back streets and stopped under some trees by a vacant lot a block away from the Taylor building.

I cut the ignition and lights and sat there in the car for ten minutes. Nothing moved. The one-man police force would be drinking coffee and kidding the waitress under the fluorescent lights three blocks away. There was no use waiting any longer. This was as nearly perfect as it would ever be. I got out and opened the trunk. Everything I'd need was in the cardboard box except the flashlight I'd bought, and I dropped that in my pocket.

A lone drop of rain splashed wetly in my face. It was so dark I could see only the faintly blacker loom of the trees against the sky. Then I could just made out the square shape of the building across the vacant lot. I was at the rear of it now. Suppose someone had discovered the unlocked window and fastened it again? Well, suppose they had? I couldn't help it now. I came around the corner and felt for the sash.

It slid upwards. Nobody had ever noticed it. I reached the box through and set it on the floor of the washroom, and then climbed in myself and pulled the window down. After feeling my way out of the little room I closed the door and sighed with relief. So far, so good, I thought.

I went up the stairs. It was hard to breathe in the hot, dead air up here under the roof. My footsteps echoed through the building as I picked my way through disordered piles of rubbish.

I set the box down against a wall and swept the light around. Anywhere would do. This was as good as any. I set the light in an old chair and opened the box, lifting out the pitch pine shavings I had whittled out that Sunday in the woods. Taking four kitchen matches out of the box, I bound them to the wire cross-arm as I had done before. Then I wound and set the clock, checking it against my watch, and wound the alarm. I set it for 12:30, and released the catch. I was sweating profusely now. The heat was almost unbearable.

I put the clock back in the box and eased the sandpaper up against the match heads, checking for just the proper tension. Then I took a folded newspaper off a pile nearby and sliced it to shreds with my knife, dropping the strips into the box over and around the clock until it was full and overflowing, dribbling dozens of matches through it as I went. I added the pine shavings and slivers, building it up. There would be no smell of oil or kerosene here when they started investigating. Of course there would be the clock, or what would be left of it, but there were already at least three or four of them in all this junk so it would probably never be noticed. The solder would melt in the intense heat and the wire cross-arm would drop off, leaving it looking just like any other discarded alarm clock except that the bell was gone. I pushed the pile of newspapers against it on one side and set some chairs on the other, then tore up more papers to pile on top of the box.

I wiped the sweat off my face and stood back to look at it in the narrow beam of the flashlight. It would do. Once those matches caught the whole rat's nest would take off like gunpowder. Well, I thought, they like to go to fires. This'll give 'em one to talk about.

When I awoke the next morning it was a minute or so

before I remembered. I began to tighten up then. When I looked at my watch I thought of that clock ticking away the seconds and the hands creeping slowly around and the fact that nothing could stop it now. It was eight o'clock, and the next four hours and a half were going to be rough. Once it was started and I got moving I should be able to shake the nervousness and keyed-up tension, but the waiting was going to be bad. I had to act naturally. I couldn't be looking at my watch every three minutes. It started off all right. As soon as I had a cup of coffee and got over to the lot, Harshaw and I got in another beef about something. God knows that was routine and natural enough. I can't even remember what this one was about. It never took much to start us off because we always reacted to each other like a couple of strange bears. And the funny part of it was that I had begun to have a sort of reluctant liking for him. He was as tough as boot-leather and he barked at everybody, but you were never in doubt as to how you stood with him. He told you. But the fact remained the more I had to admit he wasn't a bad sort of joe, the more I'd go out of my way to start a row.

"You know, Madox," he said, leaning back in his chair and sticking a match to the cold cigar. "I can't figure you out. You sell cars, but I'll be a dirty pimp if I know how you do it."

He was right. I'd hit a lucky streak the past few days and unloaded several of his jalopies. "Well," I said, "it's sure as hell not the advertising. Why don't you go ahead and build a fence around the place to keep people from finding out you've got cars in here? They keep sneaking in."

"So you sell three cars, and now you're going to tell me how to run the place?"

"I don't care what you do with it," I said, and walked out of the office. I had to relax. At this rate I'd blow my top before noon. A Negro boy came in and stood around with his hands in his pockets looking at the cars the way they always do. You get the impression they're waiting for something, but you don't know what—maybe for prices to come down or cotton to go up.

Suppose I lost my head? I thought.

I went over and gave him sales talk you'd use on an oil man looking for Cadillacs for three of his girl friends. Or at least I think it was all right. He seemed to like it. I didn't hear a word I was saying.

You can take care of everything except chance. Chance can kill you.

"How much the down payment?" he asked. That was all they ever wanted to know. You could sell Fords for eight thousand dollars if you'd let them go for five dollars down.

Somehow ten o'clock came and went. I walked over to the restaurant and had a cup of coffee. It was hard to sit still now, or stand still, or think straight about anything. At 11:45 Gulick went to get his lunch. Suppose he didn't get back in time? Harshaw would leave anyway. It would look funny if I ran off and left the place completely unattended. I prowled around the lot, trying not to look at my watch. At 12:20 he came back and Harshaw left. Then it was 12:25. I stood behind a car, looking at the watch, waiting. It was 12:30.

And nothing happened. There was no noise, no siren, nothing. The streets were as quiet as any weekday noon. It was 12:35, 12:40. It hadn't gone off. Somebody had found it. The whole thing had failed. And I couldn't try it again, if somebody had found that one. Was I glad, now that the pressure was off? I didn't know.

Then it came. The siren tore its way up through the noonday hush, growing louder and higher, screaming. The firehouse was only two blocks away, and in a minute or so the fire engine came lumbering past the lot, headed down Main, with the cars beginning to fall in behind it. Gulick and I ran to the sidewalk, both of us looking wildly around for the smoke.

"It's down there, in front of the bank somewhere!" he said, pointing. People afoot were running now, and cars were beginning to jam up down at the other end of the street.

"Stick around, and I'll go take a look," I said. Before he could answer I jumped in the car and shot out into the street. Most of the traffic and the people afoot were at least a block ahead of me. People were pouring out of stores and the restaurant, yelling at each other and running. And in the midst of all the uproar I discovered I was cold as ice and clear-headed, without any panic at all. A block before I got to the bank I turned left and pulled the car to the kerb near the mouth of the alley in the side street. Two or three other cars were parked along here, so it didn't look conspicuous. Two people went past, running, not even seeing me.

The side street was empty now. A few people still ran by on Main, but they looked straight ahead, their eyes on the smoke. I reached into the back seat. The blanket and piece of line were carefully folded up inside the coat to the seersucker suit I had put on this morning. I picked it all up, put the coat over my arm, and went down the alley, running fast. When I got to the end of it I slowed a little. A man came running past, but didn't see me, and went on up past the side door of the bank. There was nobody else in sight except the stragglers going by on Main. I went up alongside the bank building to the side door, stopped, and looked in. This was where it had to be right.

It was just the way I'd figured it. The only person in the place was the old man, and he was standing in the front door with his back to me, watching the black column of smoke boiling into the sky two blocks away. I eased inside the door, turned, and started back to the washroom, watching him with quick glances over my shoulder. The rubber-soled shoes I had on made no sound at all, and he was intent on the uproar down the street.

I made it, and slipped inside the little room, praying the door didn't squeak. I pushed it carefully until it was nearly closed, and I was out of sight. I took a deep breath. There was a half partition, presumably with a toilet behind it, and on this side were the usual wash-basin and mirror. The mirror didn't face the door. I'd already checked on that.

I put the plug in the wash-basin and turned on the water, then stepped back against the wall where I would be behind the door as he pushed it open. I hung the coat on a hook, held the blanket in my hands, and waited, hardly breathing now. It was deathly quiet. The basin filled, then started spilling over on to the floor. Suppose he was hard of hearing and didn't notice it? I cursed myself. I was doing too much supposing. A minute dragged by, and then another. Water was beginning to run out into the bank now. I turned my head and looked out the crack at the back of the door. I could see the front of the bank, only a narrow strip between here and there. He was nowhere in sight.

Then suddenly I heard the faint scuff of a shoe, just outside. He had already passed the area I was watching, was almost to the door. I wheeled around just as he stepped inside the washroom, pushing the door back towards me. He was clear of it and starting to bend over the wash-basin to turn the water off.

I hit the door with my elbow and slammed it shut at the same time I threw the blanket over him. He straightened, tried to turn, and screamed. There was no chance he had seen me. He fought the blanket wildly, trying to get his arms up. I pulled them down, took two turns around him with the line, and tied it off, then pulled his feet from under him and set him on the floor and threw two half-hitches around his ankles. He was still yelling, the sound muffled inside the blanket.

I had the knife out. I pulled the blanket away from his lower face and quickly cut a hole in it around his mouth. Grabbing a paper towel out of the container on the wall, I rolled it into a tight ball and the next time he opened his mouth to scream I shoved it inside, hard, and plastered a strip of adhesive tape across it. I straightened, and wiped the sweat off my face. It had taken a month.

He could breathe all right, but he couldn't yell. It was a lot of trouble, but if I'd tried slugging him I might have killed him. He was too old.

I opened the door a crack and peered out. It was clear. No one was in sight anywhere. I grabbed the coat and stepped out and closed the door. I was in plain sight of the street now. It was like being naked in a dream. I made it to the gate in the railing, and then I was in the vault.

Maybe I'd expected it to be full of currency stacked everywhere on the floor like cordwood. It threw me for a second. I didn't see anything except ledgers, papers, filing cabinets, and drawers. I started yanking the drawers open. Some of them were locked. I got one open at last that was full of currency in bundles, fastened with paper bands. I didn't look at the denominations. Time was running; I could feel it going past me like the tide. I jerked the undershirt out of my coat pocket; it had been tied off with a cord to form a bag, and I started cramming in the bundles.

I came out of the vault and ran up in back of the tellers' cages, bent over and hidden from the street by the ground glass screen and the counter. In another thirty seconds I'd be out of here. It was beginning to get me now. I cleaned out the first one, and moved to the other. It was just a few seconds now. Then I stopped dead still and listened, feeling the pulse jump in my throat. There was somebody on the sidewalk outside.

I dropped, squatting below the counter, trying to listen above the roaring of blood in my ears. The footsteps were going on past. Would whoever it was look inside and wonder why no one was in sight? Then I froze. I could feel the icy wind blowing right up my spine. The shuffling footsteps hadn't gone past. They had come in. Somebody was inside the bank, right on the other side of the counter.

I tried to stop the sound of my breathing. And then, in an agonizing flashback of memory, I thought of the thing I had done that day when I hadn't seen anybody here. I had looked down inside the cages.

He hadn't said anything. Why didn't something happen? I fought desperately to hold myself still, not give way to the awful compulsion to break and run for it. Then he moved again. And now I began to get it. There was another sound beside the scrape of his shoes. It was the tap, tap, tap of a cane.

"Mister Julian? You theah, Mr. Julian? Wheahbouts the fiah?"

I could feel myself weaken all over and the sigh coming up out of my lungs like a balloon collapsing. I throttled it and tried to hold my breath as I came slowly to my feet.

It was awful. It could break your nerve. We were facing each other across the counter and I was looking right into the dark glasses three feet in front of my eyes. I was robbing a bank with a witness standing there so near he could reach out and touch me, a witness who could send me to the penitentiary for practically the rest of my life except for the fact that he was blind.

"That you, Mister Julian?" he asked.

How did he know somebody was here? *Did* he know it? I didn't dare move. And I couldn't speak. That was the way he identified people, by their voices. And I couldn't stand there forever. He was reaching out an arm, groping for me. I leaned back, not moving my feet, and the fingers passed an inch away from my tie.

"Ain't like you, Mister Julian, makin' fun of ol' Mort."

I had to get out. I couldn't stand it. I moved one foot back, picking it up and lowering it carefully and utterly without sound, crêpe rubber against tile. Then I moved the other one. I repeated it. I was out of the cage. I held the bag out from my legs so I wouldn't brush against it. I was past the other cage now, in the railed-off area where the desk was.

I looked at him, and that was when I began to go to pieces. It wasn't human. He had moved. He had walked along the front of the counter and now he had stopped beside the railing, and he was tracking me. He couldn't see me, and no pair of ears on earth could have detected any sound, but he was following me as unerringly as radar. I moved, and the gaunt black face and sightless eyes moved with me.

"You got no business in heah!" he said.

I ran.

8

THE STREET WAS CLEAR, and there was no one in the alley. I got the trunk of the car open, threw in the bag, tossed the coat on the back seat, and made a U turn, throwing gravel, and shot across Main Street. This way I'd come in behind the Taylor building. They'd have the other street blocked by now, and I had to get into the thick of it without anyone's seeing me drive up. I slammed ahead two blocks and turned left.

Smoke was pouring into the sky. I hit a jam of abandoned cars, pulled over to the kerb, and got out. The crowds were all ahead of me in the street and beginning to push on to the vacant lots around the rear of the building. The fire engine was around in front, in the middle of the worse jam. I circled, keeping to the rear of the crowd. Nobody paid any attention to me. The whole second floor of the building was roaring now, throwing flames into the air. I shoved my way into the knot of people pressed around the fire engine. They had a hose run out, playing a stream on the roof on the other side, and now they were trying to get one on this side. Everybody was yelling and getting in the way. I saw the chance I was looking for and latched on to the hose, up near the nozzle, as they fought to get it strung out through the crowd.

They gave us the pressure before we got set. The hose stiffened, bucked, and threw the man who was carrying the nozzle. The man next in line went for it, got his hands on it, but he was too light and it slapped him off. Two more lunged for it. I piled into them.

"Look out!" I yelled. "Let me at the damned thing!"

I collided with one of the men, knocked him off his feet,

and then fell over him on to the hose. I was soaked, drowned, covered with churned-up mud. It was perfect. It was just what I wanted. I got both hands on the nozzle, dug my feet in, and got up. I held it, and started going forward. I could hear the crowd yell.

We had two streams on the fire now, but we might as well have been squirting a burning oil well with water pistols. The whole thing was going up like a Roman candle. A big section of the roof caved in and sparks and embers went exploding upwards in the smoke. The crowd was pushing in across the vacant lot all around us. I swung my head and through all the confusion I could see the deputy sheriff and two more men running along the line trying to force them back. I jerked my head at the two men behind me.

"Slide up here and take this!" I yelled. They clamped their hands on it and I let go, ducked back, and made for the deputy. I got him by the arm and yelled in his ear.

"That wall's coming down any minute! We got to get 'em out of here."

"What you think I'm trying to do?" he roared back.

"Look! Go tell 'em to cut the water on this hose. Then get as many men on it as you can. Pick it up. We'll shove 'em back."

He got what I meant, and ran towards the fire engine. I turned and ploughed my way back to the nozzle. Just as I got my hands on it the hose went limp. I started running, dragging it, down alongside the wall and out into the vacant lot at the rear, as far as it would reach. Men were falling in behind me now, picking it up. I started swinging it out and away, like hauling a fish seine. The deputy was yelling and motioning backwards with his arms. They began to back up, and every time they gave a step we dragged the hose against them. In a couple of minutes we had the whole crowd shoved back across the street.

The wall didn't fall outwards after all. It sagged a little and went on burning. But I had accomplished the thing I wanted. That deputy, and at least a half dozen others, would remember me all right. My clothes were a mess; I looked as if I'd been fighting fire for a week. There wasn't much to do now except to keep it from spreading to the houses along the street. We put out fires in the weeds and sprayed water on some of the nearer shacks. And all the time I was waiting. It would break any minute now.

Then I heard a siren, pitched low and merely growling. Another highway patrol car was inching its way through the crowd jammed in the street. The driver got out and waved his arm towards the deputy sheriff. The deputy went over, while people pressed around them. Then I saw some of them break away and start running towards Main.

I shoved into the knot of men. The word was travelling faster than another fire. "What's up?" I yelled at a man squeezing his way out.

"Bunch of men held up the bank! While everybody was over here at the fire they stuck it up and got away with ten thousand dollars!"

"Did they catch 'em?" I tried to grab his arm.

"Not yet. They got away in a car." He was gone past me.

By the time I got back to the lot it had grown to four men with sub-machine guns and thirty thousand dollars, and the car was a black sedan. I didn't pay much attention to it. This was the kind of rumour you'd expect; the men who were working from facts, over there at the bank, wouldn't be saying what they'd found out. It was just a matter of time till they got the hunch the fire was rigged and start at it from that angle. As far as I could see it had come off without a hitch; I hadn't left a track.

The letdown began to catch up with me. I told them I was going over to the room to change clothes. What I really needed was a drink. As soon as I got out of the shower I dug the bottle out of the suitcase, poured a stiff slug in a glass, and collapsed on the side of the bed. It had been rough. I had lost all track of time. I took a jolt of the whisky, felt it explode inside me, and wondered how much money there was out there in the trunk of the car. I couldn't even guess.

I went back to the lot. The whole town was in an uproar. It was the biggest thing since V-J Day. The Sheriff and two more deputies had just arrived from the county seat twenty miles away. Highways were being blockaded in all adjoining counties. The story was already spreading across town that the fire had been a decoy. The next rumour was that two experts from the insurance company were already on their way up from Houston. Well, they'd have a hard time proving it, and if they did they wouldn't be much better off except that it'd point a little more to somebody here in town.

It was hard on the nerves, thinking of that money still in the trunk of the car, but the only thing I could do was ride it out until after dark. I went up and mixed with the crowd gawking round the bank. Julian was all right, they said. He hadn't been hurt, just a little shaken up and scared. He was inside there now, with the police. But he couldn't give any description of the man, or men; all he'd seen was a blanket flopping down over his head. He hadn't heard any voices, though; which might mean there'd been only one man. Old Mort, the Negro, was a sensation. He'd been so close to one of the robbers he could hear him breathing. He was that close, he said, measuring with his hands. He could of reached out and touched him.

I sweated out the afternoon some way, and after it was dark I eased out of town, driving south on the highway. Nobody stopped me, or even seemed to notice. Before I turned off on to the dirt road I looked back for lights. There was nobody behind me. The moon wasn't up yet, and it was partly overcast and very dark. Just before I got to the abandoned farm up on the sandhill among the pines, I pulled off and cut my lights. I wasn't being followed. When my eyes were accustomed to the darkness I pulled back into the road and went on. At the gate I turned sharply left and went on around behind the old sagging barn and stopped the car where it would be out of sight of anyone going past out in front.

Fighting the impatience, I waited a few minutes to be sure. Nuts, I thought; there's nobody within miles. I got out, opened the trunk, and carried the bag inside the barn before I switched on the flashlight. My hands were beginning to tremble a little and I was conscious of a wild excitement. I went inside the corn crib and closed the door. I didn't notice the heat now, or the sweat on my face. I upended the bag and let the bundles and loose bills cascade on to the floor. It was wonderful.

I didn't try to count all of it. Most of the bundles were fifties, twenties, and tens. Without any of the loose bills or the ones it came to $12,300. I whistled softly. A wild impatience began to get hold of me. I wanted to get going, to put it back in the car and run.

Run where? I thought.

The world wouldn't hold me, and I knew it. It wouldn't take them an hour to figure it out if I disappeared now. They could add too. I couldn't leave. The only way I could beat them was the one I'd known from the first, and that was to keep my head down and wait it out. After a month or so, when the heat began to die down . . . I gathered the bag up and went out the door of the crib.

Picking a spot near the rear wall of the crib, inside one of the stalls, I scraped the old manure out of the way with a piece of shingle, and started to dig. The ground was sand, and easy to gouge up with the shingle. I was careful to place all the loose dirt in one pile. When I was down about eighteen inches, I rolled the bag of money into as tight a ball as I could make it, and shoved it into the hole. Then, just before I started scooping the dirt back in, I thought of something. I lifted it out and began looking over the undershirt. There was a laundry mark on it, all right. Taking out my knife, I sawed out the piece of cloth and stuck a match to it, then ground the ashes into the bottom of the hole. If anybody did happen to stumble on to it I'd lose the money, but they'd never tie it to me.

I put it back in the hole and began filling it, tamping the dirt down with my fist until it was as firm as the rest of the ground. The little which was left over I spread evenly around, then raked the dried manure and old straw back over the whole area.

Snapping off the light, I went back to the door. The old house was just a faintly darker shadow in the night, off there to the left, and as I looked towards it I thought for the hundredth time of that other day and what Sutton had said to her and the way she detested and feared him. There was something insane about it. You could keep trying for years to add it up and you'd never come out with an answer that made sense. She wouldn't even *know* Sutton. The hell she didn't——!

I shook them off angrily. What business was it of mine? But, as always, when I gathered her up and threw her out of my mind there was a little of her left over, the way there is in a room a girl has just walked through.

I went out and got in the car, but instead of heading right back to town I drove on down to the river and went swimming by the bridge. When I did go back I stopped in at the restaurant to get a cup of coffee. The waitress looked at my head and smiled.

"What's the matter?" I asked. "Did I forget to put on my hair?"

She grinned. "No. But it looks like you left it out in the rain."

"I been swimming," I said. "They caught the bank robbers yet?"

"No. But they got enough cops around here to catch Dillinger."

"You don't even remember Dillinger," I said. "You were just a kid in a three-cornered Bikini."

She laughed, tickled about it. I went back to the rooming house, took another drink, and lay down on the bed, feeling the tension go out of me. I was in. The money was buried, and I hadn't left a track behind me.

The next day was Saturday, but there wasn't much business transacted. They might as well have closed the whole town except that there wouldn't have been any places for people to congregate and rehash the robbery. The place was full of cops. The white-haired Sheriff from the county seat was in town with two of his deputies besides the one who lived here, and there were some more with plain-clothes cop written all over them, probably from the detective agency or insurance company. Everybody was wild to get at the remains of the fire and start pawing through it for evidence, but a lot of it was still smouldering and too hot. Special deputies had been sworn in to keep people away from the place. I had a hunch the Sheriff and the detectives had already junked the out-of-town gang idea and were playing it cagey, going through the motions of looking for the getaway car while they waited for somebody to stick his head up or make a slip. That much money would be burning somebody's pockets and he'd have to start throwing it around. All right, I thought; go ahead. I know about that one too.

All I had to do was keep playing it down the middle. I stuck around the lot and talked robbery with anybody who drifted in. And then Harshaw pulled a funny one on me. Around noon he called me into the office. He was chewing a cold cigar and oiling a big salt-water reel on his desk.

"Sit down," he said. "I want to talk to you."

I perched on the side of a desk, wondering what was coming. "What's up?" I asked, as casually as I could.

"I want you to take charge here for a while. My wife and I are going to Galveston for a week."

"What's the matter with Gulick?" I asked.

"There's nothing the matter with Gulick," he said impatiently. "Except that he's a little slow and he won't take responsibility. You can use your own judgment about trades. Do you want it, or don't you?"

"O.K. with me," I said. For once I couldn't start an argument.

"You can run an ad if you want to," he said. "The paper comes out early in the week."

"What'll I use for money? My own?"

He sighed and shook his head. "You're a tough nut to get along with, Madox. Why in hell would I ask you to pay for the ad out of your pocket? They can send the bill to Miss Harper. Or tell her to give it to you out of petty cash."

"O.K.," I said. At least he was taking that over-ripe bundle of sex with him this time.

He finished cleaning the reel and put it in a flannel bag

with a drawstring. "Well, if you can't think of anything else to bitch about, I'll leave it with you," he said, starting out the door.

"What are you going after?" I asked. "Tarpon?"

"No. Hammerhead sharks. They got some big ones around the jetties down there."

After I came back from lunch I went out on the lot and picked out about a half-dozen cars that would make good leaders in an ad, made some notes, and started writing it up. At first I was just doing it to kill time, but the thing began to grow on me as I went along and after the second or third draft I had some pretty good stuff whipped into shape, slicing the down payments as low as they would go and playing up all the accessories. I took it up the street to the newspaper office, paid for it and got a receipt, intending to go by the loan office and collect from Gloria Harper.

I had started back to the office before I remembered it was Saturday and they closed at noon. Well, I could collect on Monday; it didn't matter. But I was conscious of a vague disappointment, and knew the money was only part of it; what I'd really wanted was an excuse to go in and talk to her.

I was angling across the street towards the lot when I happened to glance around towards the loan office and saw her through the window. She was sitting at a desk behind a pile of paper work. I turned abruptly and started back, and just as I did I noticed that Gulick had company on the lot. Two of the deputy sheriffs were talking to him.

Well, it wasn't anything. They were talking to everybody in town. There was nothing unusual about it. But still I wished I hadn't turned right there in the middle of the street; it might look as if I had turned back to avoid them. But there wasn't anything I could do about it now. If I kept switching back and forth in the middle of the street I would *attract* attention.

The door was open and there was a big electric fan blowing across the office. She nodded as I came in, but the smile itself was a little forced and there was something very tired about her face. I wondered why she was working overtime.

She got up and came over to the counter with tall un-hurried grace.

"It was terrible about the bank, wasn't it?" she said. "And the fire."

"Yes," I said. I wasn't even thinking about the bank. And then I remembered what I had come in for. "Harshaw said to take it out of petty cash," I said, shoving the receipt across the counter and explaining what it was for.

She wrote out a slip and got the money out of the safe. "Thanks," I said, putting it into my wallet. "Why don't you knock off? You look tired."

"I will pretty soon."

I didn't want to go. We stood there facing each other across the counter. "What are you going to do tomorrow?" I asked.

"Nothing special. Go to church in the morning, I expect. And in the afternoon I thought I might go out and try to sketch the Buchanan bridge."

"Where's that?"

"It's in the river bottom, below the one where——" She paused, confused, and I knew what she was thinking. "Below the one we crossed going out to the oil well."

"Could I go, too?" I asked.

She nodded. "Why, yes. We could make it a picnic."

"That's fine. I'll get the restaurant to make us a lunch to take along."

'No. Let me do that," she said. "It's no trouble."

"What time can I pick you up?"

"About twelve would be all right."

"Great," I said. "I'll be looking forward to it."

I started out and then paused, when I reached the door-way, to look back at her. She was still watching me, and had just started to turn back to the desk.

It was awkward, somehow. Both of us were a little con-fused. "Was— I mean, is there anything else?" she asked.

"Oh," I said. "No. I guess not." I turned and went on out into the street.

When I got over to the lot the two deputies were gone and Gulick didn't say anything about them.

I DROVE OVER around noon. It was a blazing, still day of white sunlight, and the shadows under the trees were like pools of ink. She was sitting on the front porch waiting for me, dressed in white shorts and a blue T-shirt, and surrounded by painting equipment and the box of lunch. I got out and loaded it all into the back seat. The cocker spaniel was running eagerly up and down the walk.

"Can we take Spunky?" she asked. "He likes to run rabbits."

I looked at Spunky's short legs and big paddle feet. "Did he ever catch one?"

She smiled. "No. But he's still hopeful."

"Sure," I said. I lifted him in through the rear window and held the door open for her. As we went down Main Street a few people were clustered in front of the drugstore and the restaurant.

"They're still talking about the bank robbery," she said. "Do you think it was somebody around here?"

I didn't want to talk about it. "I don't know," I said. "It could have been."

When we were on the highway going south I cranked the wing windows open and swung them around front to scoop in a little breeze. She sat back in the corner of the seat, facing towards me with one leg doubled under her, and the big violet eyes were happier than I had ever seen them before.

The road was a mile or so beyond the one which went over to Sutton's oil well. It wasn't much more than a pair of ruts struggling through the sand and stunted postoak in a generally westerly direction towards the river bottom, and looked as if it hadn't been used in months.

"Where's it go?" I asked.

"Nowhere, any more. The bridge isn't safe and it's all washed out beyond, on the other side of the bottom. We can get as far as the bridge, though."

When we got down among the big oaks in the bottom there was more shade and it was a little cooler. The road wound erratically, skirting the dried-up sloughs. Once we almost ran over an old boar which came charging out of some bushes into the road ahead of us.

"That looked like a wild pig," I said.

"Some of them are," she said. "They get lost down here and after a while they sort of go native."

"You'd better warn Spunky they're not rabbits. They could slice him up like salami."

When we finally got to the river it was worth it, and I could see why she had wanted to come here. It was beautiful and remote and there was a feeling of peace about it as if they'd forgotten to wind the clock and it had run down fifty years ago. There was no concrete or steel about the bridge; it was a sagging ruin of oak timbers and loose planking weathered to the bleached-out whiteness of old bones against the dark wall of timber beyond it, and tilted a little as if it would go out with the next high water. There was a jam of whitened logs on the upper side and the water ran dark, almost like black tea, out from under the jam, boiling up a little and swinging around in a big hole on the downriver side. The road approached from below the bridge and where I pulled the car off and stopped in the shade of a huge pin oak there was a clean sandy bank sloping down to the sandbar below the pool.

She looked across the river and then at me. "It's lovely, isn't it?"

"It's perfect," I said.

We got out. Spunky ran down to the sandbar to get a drink and then took off to investigate the surrounding country. I took the water jar down to the river's edge and filled it for her, and when I came back she was looking around for a place to sit down in the shade.

"Wait," I said, "I've got——" And then I chopped it off suddenly, feeling cold chills down my back. I'd almost said blanket. It had been a near thing, and thinking about it scared me.

She looked at me questioningly. "What is it?"

I got hold of myself. "Nothing," I said. "False alarm. I started to say I had a Sunday paper in the car that you could sit on, but I just remember I didn't bring it."

"Oh," she said, "I don't need anything. This is nice sand, just like a beach."

She sat down with the block of paper on her legs and took up one of the charcoal sticks, looking meditatively at the bridge. Then she glanced around at me where I'd stretched out on the sand, just smoking a cigarette and watching her.

"Do I make you nervous?" I asked. "Watching you, I mean?"

She shook her head. "No. But I was just thinking you'd probably be awfully bored."

"Take my word for it," I said, looking at the lovely face and the big, serious eyes. "I'm not bored."

"You know, you're awfully nice," she said quietly. "You're not at all like I thought you were at first. I——" She broke off and looked out over the bridge. "I mean, does that sound like too shameless a thing to say?"

"You're a solid brass hussy," I said.

She smiled, trying to cover up the confusion in her face. "Don't make fun of me, please. What I'm trying to say is that you *have* been nice and the least I could do is acknowledge it, after the mean things I thought about you at first."

I rolled on my side and propped myself on my elbow. "I told you how that happened. I just got the instructions mixed up. This is Approach No. 2, known as the waiting game. You want me to explain how it works? You take these two citizens, A and B, we'll call 'em——"

She laughed, and picked up the charcoal stick again. "All

right. I've been warned. But didn't your instruction book warn you?"

"About what?" I asked.

"That your Approach No. 2, as you call it, won't work after it's been explained."

"Killjoy. Now I've got to buy a new manual."

She laughed again and started blocking in the outline of the bridge with the charcoal. I lay there and watched her, thinking how beautiful she was, and about the joking, and then beginning to be aware that beneath it there was something serious that had nothing to do with joking at all. I wondered if she had felt it too. What was there about this kid that kept getting under my skin? And then I wondered irritably why I kept insisting on thinking of her as a kid. She was twenty-one. I was nine years older than she was, but that didn't mean she was sixteen any more.

It was impossible to lie there and watch her sketching without thinking of that other time at the abandoned farm, and that put me right back on the same old merry-go-round with Sutton and the same old unanswerable questions. But I had my mind made up about one thing—I wasn't going to ask her about it again, at least not today. We were having too much fun, and the mention of Sutton always spoiled it for her. Maybe some day she would tell me.

What the hell, some day? In a month—or two, at the most—I'd be gone from here. As soon as the heat was off a little and the bank job began gathering dust in the unsolved file I'd dig up the money and beat it.

She was squeezing colours on to the plate from little tubes, and dipping her brush into the water jar to mix them.

"I thought watercolours came in little blocks," I said.

"They do," she said. "But the tubes are better."

Just then Spunky came flopping down the bank, soaking wet and plastered with sand, and bounced in between us. I saw what was coming and grabbed him before he could get the shake started, rolling over and tossing him down below us.

She laughed. "That was fast work."

"He'd have made a Navajo sand painting out of it in about one more second."

"You're nice to have around. Every painter should have one of you."

"It'd never work out," I said. "You run into the same old distribution problems. The pretty ones would soon corner the market."

"You're very flattering today."

"It's probably just the moonlight."

She wrinkled her nose at me and went on with her brush. She worked fast, and I watched the picture take form. I knew nothing whatever about painting, of course, but it looked fine to me. It wasn't exactly like the bridge, but somehow it had that same drowsy feeling of peace.

"I like that," I said. "Will you do one for me sometime?"

She didn't look up. "Have you wondered who this one is for?"

"You mean I can have it?"

"If you'd like it."

"Of course I would. But why?"

"I don't know," she said quietly. "Maybe just because it's my birthday, and I wanted to give you something."

"That sounds crazy somewhere," I said. "But is it really your birthday?"

She nodded, and put down the brush and set the block of paper off her legs on to the sand. "I'll finish it later. Why don't we eat our lunch now? I'll show you my birthday cake."

I went up and got the box out of the car and we started unpacking it, putting the sandwiches and Thermos jugs out on the tablecloth on the sand. She lifted out a small tin candy-box.

"You open it," she said.

I lifted the lid. There was a small cake inside, not much bigger than an overgrown cupcake, covered with white frosting and dotted with what looked like round sections cut out of dates.

"They're instead of candles," she said.

"Twenty-two?" I asked.

She smiled and shook her head. "You remembered, didn't you? But it's twenty-one. I mean, when you asked me, it was so near——"

"Child," I said. "Twenty-and-a-half years old."

I must have looked disappointed, or something. "What's the matter?" she asked. "Did you want me to be twenty-two?"

"No," I said. "That would be stupid, wouldn't it?"

"Yes," she answered quietly. "Wouldn't it?"

"I'm thirty."

"Well, have a sandwich, you poor old man, to keep up your strength."

"Wait," I said. "We can't eat sandwiches until we drink a toast." I opened one of the Thermos jugs and filled two aluminium cups. It was iced tea.

"To Gloria," I said, "who is twenty-one all the time and beautiful in the moonlight."

I don't know what happened to the rest of the afternoon. We ate the lunch, and then she worked some more on the picture. We couldn't go swimming because neither of us had brought a suit, but we took off our shoes and went wading out on the sandbar. Sometime during the afternoon a big swamp rabbit came bounding downriver with Spunky yelping along in his wake and falling farther behind at every jump, and then the next thing we knew the sun was gone. It had dropped out of sight behind the timber and the shadows were long and growing darker out across the bottom.

"I had no idea it was so late," she said. "We'll have to go. I promised I'd stay with Gloria Two while they went to Bible Class."

We gathered up the painting equipment and the lunch box and stowed them in the car, and it wasn't until we were almost ready to get in ourselves that we realized Spunky was missing. Neither of us could recall seeing him since he'd gone past chasing the rabbit.

We began calling him, but he didn't come. I walked up-

river a few hundred yards, and then down, calling and
whistling, but there was no sign of him. When I got back to
the car it was growing dark, and I could see she was worried and a little frightened. I could have kicked myself for
what I'd said about the wild hogs.

"Harry, do you suppose something has happened to
him?" she asked anxiously.

"He'll show up," I said. "He's all right."

"But it's getting dark. I'm scared for him."

"He can follow his own backtrail. I'm not concerned
about that. But I've got to take you home. Your family'll be
worried about you."

"But we can't just go off and leave poor Spunky down
here alone——"

"I'll find him," I said. "You just get in the car. And then
give me your shoes."

She looked at me wonderingly. "My shoes? But why?"

I grinned. "I want something you're wearing, and I can't
think of anything else you can spare without starting a
riot."

"Oh," she said. She sat down on the seat and slipped off
the wedgies. They had grass straps, and it suddenly
occurred to me they were the same as the ones Dolores
Harshaw wore. I took them back and put them down on the
sand where we'd eaten lunch, and then got in the car.

"We're just going to leave them there?" she asked,
puzzled.

"Yes. And when I get back, Spunky should be asleep with
his head on them. It's an old trick. When you lose a dog,
leave something he knows is yours at the last place he saw
you. When he comes back he'll wait by it."

I wasn't nearly as optimistic about it as I pretended, but
there was nothing else we could do at the moment. My
experience when I was a boy had been with hunting dogs—
bird dogs and hounds—and as far as I knew these house-
bred fluffballs like Spunky might be as helpless in the
woods as bubble-dancers.

She was very quiet as we drove back to town. They were
waiting on the front porch and you could see they had been

worried about her. There was a great deal of excited talk while she tried to explain the shoe trick and why she was barefoot, and then Gloria Two began to cry when she realized Spunky was lost. Robinson wanted to go with me to help look for him when I went back, but I told him it wasn't necessary. For some reason I wanted to do it alone.

It was slow going, driving back over that road at night, and it was nearly nine o'clock before I got to the bridge. As I made the last turn I expected to see Spunky come bounding into the headlights, overjoyed at seeing somebody again, but the river bank was deserted and silent as it had been when we left. I got out and walked down to where I'd left her shoes. He wasn't there. I began to be worried about it then. There was no telling what had happened to him. There were thousands and thousands of acres of wild river bottom down here and if he didn't have any sense of direction or a good nose he might never find his way back.

I picked the shoes up and took them back to the car, suddenly conscious of the presence of Gloria Harper in everything connected with this place and with the whole happy afternoon which had slipped past us so quickly. She was everywhere. I wanted to see her now—but how could I go back and face her without the dog? She would be desolate because Gloria Two was heartbroken and . . .

For God's sake, I thought angrily, how silly can you get? I had a sudden, sharp, and contemptuous picture of Harry Madox at the age of thirty struggling to keep from drowning in all this sea of blonde heartbreak over a paddle-footed mop of a dog.

I didn't leave, though. I called myself eighteen different kinds of a fool, but I stayed and began calling and whistling. I cut the light after a while to keep from running the battery down, and sat there in the dark smoking cigarettes in the intervals when I wasn't yelling. It was ten o'clock, and then ten-thirty. I'd waste another half hour, and then I'd go back.

I had made a last series of whistles and was about to give up when I heard him. He was barking a short distance downriver. I walked back away from the car and yelled,

"Here, Spunky! Here, boy!" and then I saw the shadowy movement across the sand as he ran towards me. He was scared stiff and whining and trying to climb all over me. I picked him up and opened the car door to turn on the ceiling light, and looked him over to see if he'd been snake bitten. He was all right, or appeared to be, except that he was covered with mud.

I shoved him in the back and climbed in myself. He leaned up on the back of the seat and began licking me on the ear while I tried to light a cigarette. I swore at him, but it didn't do any good, and I finally gave up. I was glad too. Now I wouldn't have to go back and tell her I couldn't find him.

The house was dark when I pulled up in front. I knew they'd have returned from Bible Class by this time, so I supposed they were all in bed. They were—all except one. I had just climbed out of the car when she came out the gate, a blur in the darkness in some kind of long, pale housecoat. I knew she had been sitting up waiting for me on the porch.

"Here's your friend," I said, pitching my voice down so I wouldn't wake them up. I scooped him out of the back of the car and dropped him over the fence. When I turned back she was standing beside me and quite near, and my eyes were becoming accustomed to the darkness so I could see her face. Her eyes were very big and they looked black in the starlight, and her hair was a rumpled mop of blondeness.

"It was wonderful of you," she whispered.

"Not at all."

"I was worried; you were gone so long."

We were whispering like a boy and girl in a doorway. "He wasn't there. I had to keep calling him. But he's all right; he was just lost."

"I was afraid you were lost."

"You were?"

"Yes," she said quietly. "Thank you for everything. It was a lovely day, wasn't it?"

"Is it midnight yet?"

"Not quite."

"Well, happy birthday, Junior." I took her face in my hands and kissed her. And then they dynamited the dam.

She wasn't Junior any more and nobody was kidding and the light touch was gone somewhere downriver in the night. Her arms were around my neck and I was holding her so tightly she could hardly breathe. It was crazy and very wonderful. We didn't say anything. After a long time I let go of her and took her face in my hands again and tilted it up a little, and she put her hands up over mine. I could see the starshine in her eyes as if they were wet.

"It was a wonderful day, wasn't it?" she asked softly.

"And getting better," I said.

"I've got to go in, Harry."

"I can't let you go."

"I'll see you in the morning." Suddenly she pulled my head down and kissed me and slipped away inside the gate. "Good night, Harry," she said. I watched until she was up on the front porch and then when I heard the screen door open and close I got in the car and drove off.

I don't know how long I drove around, or where I went. Everything was mixed up and I couldn't sort it out. Once I remembered standing beside the car somewhere on a dark country road smoking and grinding a cigarette butt under my foot and thinking: I'm thirty years old and she's just a kid—just a big-eyed, beautiful kid who never says much. That's all she is. And kissing her is like driving into a nitro truck.

It must have been after two when I got back to the rooming house. I was still in the dream, and only half noticed the strange car parked at the kerb on the other side of the street. I cut my lights and got out, and then the spot hit me right in the eyes.

"Madox?" The voice came from the wall of darkness somewhere on my right.

"It's him." That one was on the left.

I couldn't see anything but the light, and cold was running up my back like a stream of ice water. But somehow I got my mind back in time from the rosy cloud it was in, and I had sense enough not to try to run. I froze up tight and waited.

"Yeah," I said, trying to make my voice sound natural. "I'm Madox. What is it?"

"We're from the Sheriff's office. You better come along with us."

10

IT WAS TOUGH, with that light in my face. I couldn't let anything show. Just hang on, I thought desperately. Play it dumb. Play it a line at a time till you find out.

"I don't get it," I said, as naturally as I could. "You want to see me? You must have the wrong party."

"We don't think so." They came out of the light then, one on each side of me. I recognized them. They were the two deputies who had been talking to Gulick Saturday afternoon. "Let's take a ride."

"Well, sure," I said. "But how's for telling me what this is all about?"

"Bank robbery—and arson," the short one said.

"Bank robbery?" I said. "Aren't you guys reaching for it a little? Look, I'm a car salesman. I work for George Harshaw——"

"We know all about that," he said, cutting me off. "But we want to have a little talk with you. I'd advise you to come along without any argument; you're just making it tough on yourself."

"Sure. If I can help you any way, I'll be glad to." I shrugged.

He came over behind me and felt me under the arms and down the sides. "He's clean, Buck," he said to the other one, and then to me, "All right, Madox. Get in the car."

"O.K.," I said. "But wait'll I lock mine."

"We'll do it. You got your keys?"

"Yeah."

"Let me have 'em."

I gave him the keys, which were still in my hand. He tossed them to the tall deputy, the one called Buck, who went around in back of the car and opened the trunk. He switched on a long-barrelled flashlight and looked over every inch of it. Then he went inside the car and began lifting up the seats and pawing through the junk in the glove compartment.

"Where you been?" the short one asked me while Buck was shaking down the car. "Two-thirty's a little late for this town."

"Just riding around," I said. "It's too hot to sleep."

"Things on your mind, maybe?" He managed to get a lot of suggestion into it. "Just where you been riding around?"

"Hell, I don't know," I said, suddenly realizing I had no idea where I'd been. "Just around. Up the highway and back."

"Maybe you'd better try to remember. You don't look too good, right now."

Just then Buck slammed the door and came over to us. "What you doing with a pair of girl's shoes in your car?" he asked.

I stared at him. Shoes? Then I remembered; I hadn't given them to her. "Oh," I said. "They belong to a friend of mine."

"She always leave her shoes in the car?" Buck asked, "I've heard of 'em leaving their pants around here and there——"

"Take it easy, Mac," I said. I told them about losing the dog and going back to find him. They motioned me towards the police car while I was talking and we got in, all three of us in the back seat. There was another man in front, at the wheel.

"And what girl was this?" the short one asked.

"Her name's Gloria Harper."

"She live here in town?"

"It's all right," the man in front said. I knew who he was then. He was the deputy who'd been at the fire, the one who lived here. "I know her. She's a nice kid. If this guy's mixed up in something I doubt if she is."

We went on through town and north on the highway. It was about twenty miles to the county seat. I was still flying blind, but I was beginning to have a hunch they were too. Maybe they didn't have a thing to go on except the fact that I was a stranger in town.

I began to breathe a little easier. So far I hadn't made a false move or spilled anything, in spite of the suddenness of it, and now that I was on guard all I had to do was play it as it turned up and stick to my story. I even had my alibi there in the front seat, the deputy who'd seen me at the fire. The only thing I had to remember was not to spring it too soon in the game. Let it come out naturally—that was the thing.

When we got into town we drove right to the jail. The Sheriff was there waiting for us in a hot, bleak office full of harsh light and steel filing cabinets. It was the first time I'd seen him up close, and I didn't much like what I saw. There wasn't any of the pot-bellied court-house stooge here; he was a policeman doing police work. The hair must have been prematurely white because the face was that of a man in his forties, a face with all the flabby indecision of the front side of an axe.

"What took you so long?" he asked Buck.

"He was out ridin' around," Buck said.

"Where?"

It was the short deputy who answered. "He says he don't know." He grinned.

I turned and looked at him. He wasn't over five feet five, with a deformed left hand and a nasty pair of eyes, and you could see he liked going around with the badge and gun as much as he didn't like men bigger than he was. The other two—Buck and the one who'd been at the fire—looked harmless enough, just lanky, serious-minded country boys drawing a county paycheque.

"All right, all right," the Sheriff said. "You and Buck can go home." They went out and he jerked his head towards a folding chair over against the wall. "Sit down, Madox," he said, taking a cigar out of a box.

I sat down. The big unshaded bulb hanging in the middle of the room made it even hotter than it was inside. I fished out a cigarette and lighted it, throwing the match into a dirty spittoon. Sweat ran down my chest inside the shirt. How much did they know?

"What's this all about, Sheriff?" I asked.

He bit the end off the cigar and looked over at the deputy, ignoring me. "What about the car, Tate?"

"It was clean. Wasn't nothing in it but a pair of girl's shoes and the junk in the glove locker. The usual stuff."

"And his room?"

Tate shook his head. "Nothing there but his clothes." He sat astride the chair with his arms propped on the back, watching me while he smoked a cigarette.

The Sheriff jerked his head around suddenly, and the cold, incisive eyes bored into me. "All right, Madox; where'd you hide it?"

"Hide what?" I asked.

"That money."

"Look, Sheriff," I said. "I could ask you what money, and waste some more of your time and mine, but I understand that I'm supposed to have robbed a bank. Is that right?"

"That's right."

"Well, let's get down to cases. I didn't rob a bank. I happen to be a car salesman, and I haven't got any sidelines. But if you think there's any way I can help you, let's get on with it and quit horsing around so I can get back and get some sleep. I've got to work tomorrow."

"O.K.," he said. He leaned backwards across the desk and flipped open one of the drawers. His hand came out holding a cardboard box. He lifted the lid off, then walked over and handed it to me. I looked at it and had to fight to keep my face still. It was the alarm clock.

"Where'd you buy it, Madox?"

"I didn't."

"You know what it is, don't you?" He didn't raise his voice or threaten. He didn't have to. He just looked at you.

"Sure," I said. "It looks like what's left of a clock." It was black, and the glass was melted.

"That's right. It's an alarm clock. Take a good look at it. See anything funny about it?"

"Nothing except that it's been on fire. But what's it got to do with me? I thought you said I robbed a bank. You mean when I got rich I burned my alarm clock?"

"Not exactly. Notice something else funny about it? It hasn't got a bell."

"All right," I said. "I'll bite. So it *hasn't* got a bell."

"Not much use as an alarm clock, is it?"

"I shouldn't think so. But I still don't get it. Why tell me?"

"Why? Just in case you ever wanted to hold up a bank sometime, and needed a diversion. It's an old Indian-fighter's trick. You'd use a clock like this to start a fire somewhere at exactly the time you wanted it started. That'd take the pressure off, because everybody in town'd go to the fire. You notice those little drops of metal on top of the clapper? They're solder. The insurance investigator who dug it out of the ashes told me about them. There was a match-holder of some kind fastened on there and it melted off with the heat, but it didn't quite *all* melt off. But it's still a damned smart trick." Suddenly he stopped his pacing back and forth and snapped at me like a popping whip. *"Madox, where'd you buy that clock?"*

"I told you," I said. "I never saw it before."

He went back and sat down on the edge of the desk. "A man smart enough to pull off a job like that'd be too smart to buy the stuff he needed for it there in town. He'd go somewhere else and get it." He leaned forward a little with the cigar in his mouth. "Now, let's have the truth for once. Where'd you go the Friday before the fire?"

I stared at him a little blankly. "Go? I don't remember going anywhere—— No, wait a minute. I did, too. I don't remember whether it was Friday or not, but about a week before the fire I went down to Houston."

"That's more like it. And what'd you go down there for? Not to buy a clock, by any chance?"

"No. I went down there to try to collect some money a man owed me."

"What man?"

"His name's Kelvey. Tom Kelvey." I was in the clear on

that. Kelvey'd owed me two hundred dollars for over a year.

"What's his address?"

I told him.

"And you saw him? And got the money?"

"No," I said. "I didn't see him."

"Well, that's too bad. You drove all the way down there to put the bite on him and then you didn't even see him. I'll bet he was out of town, wasn't he? Funny how those things happen."

I could see that one coming. They'd probably check Kelvey, so I had to do better than that. "No," I said. "I don't know whether he was home or not. I didn't even look him up."

"I see. You suddenly decided you didn't want the money after all."

"No. I got side-tracked."

"By what?"

"I ran into an old girl friend."

"And that was more important?"

"Well," I said, "you know how it is. It's always more important than anything, at the time."

"All right. Who was the girl?"

"End of the line," I said. "She's an old girl friend, like I said. But she's also married."

"Then you *did* go down there to buy a clock."

"Think anything you want. I've told you how it happened."

"But you won't say who the girl was?"

"Of course not. You think I want her to get in trouble?"

"Well, you've got yourself in trouble."

"I don't think so. You say you *think* I robbed a bank. That's not trouble, unless I'd actually done it. What'd you do, pick my name out of a hat?"

"No. This is Monday morning, and six of us have been working on this since Friday evening. It doesn't take that long to pull a name out of a hat. Madox, you might as well face it. You stick out in this thing like a cootch dancer at a funeral."

"Why?" I asked. I wiped the sweat off my face. "For God's sake, why? Because I was there in town?"

"I'm coming to that. Why were you?"

"I told you. I work there. I sell cars."

"I know. And in less than three weeks after you show up, the bank is robbed. Where'd you work last?"

"In Houston."

"So you leave a city the size of Houston and just happen to wind up in a one-horse burg of less than three thousand. To sell cars, you say. Why?"

"Cars are sold everywhere."

"Did somebody recommend the place? Did Harshaw advertise for a salesman in the Houston papers?"

"No," I said. "I——"

"I see. Just a coincidence."

"If you'll give me a chance, I'll tell you. After I quit my job in Houston, I decided I'd go to Oklahoma City. I stopped in Lander to get some lunch, and while I was eating Harshaw came in for coffee. We got to talking about something that was in the paper there on the counter, and struck up kind of a general conversation. When he found out I was a salesman, he offered me a job. You can ask him about it if you don't believe me."

"So you took a job? Just like that?"

"Why not? A job was what I was looking for."

"And then in less than three weeks somebody sticks up a bank that hasn't been robbed in the forty-three years it's been there. A week before it happens you go off somewhere for a whole day and night and you can't explain. And the same day it happens, a little after dark, you sneak out of town again for two or three hours. Where'd you go that time?"

I began to be afraid of him then. He was like a bulldog; every time he shifted his grip he got a little more of your throat.

"Well?" The relentless eyes wouldn't leave my face. "Another married woman you can't tell us about?"

"No," I said. "I remember what you're talking about. I went swimming."

"Everybody else in town is in an uproar about a fire and bank robbery, but you go swimming. All right, where'd you go?"

I told him.

"Did you ever go swimming out there at night before?"

"Yes. Several times."

He grunted. "Good. That's what I wanted to know. Now tell me something I'm curious about." He paused a moment, watching me and letting me wait. "On these other times, *did you always make it a point to stop in at the restaurant on your way back with your hair plastered down like a wet rat, and kid the waitress about it?*"

I was groggy for a minute. How could I have known I'd run into a mind like this? I'd done it deliberately, for an alibi, but he could smell it. It was overdone for him. It was phony; it stuck out. I rolled with it, trying to keep my face from showing I was being hurt.

"Look," I said, "how the hell do I know where I went every time I came back from swimming? I don't keep a diary. God, you just go swimming. And then you go home. Or you want a cup of coffee. Or a Coke. Or you go to the movies. Or to the can. Who's going to keep track of all that?"

"I was just curious about it. We'll call it another coincidence. Let's go back to the first time you were ever in that bank. You opened an account, remember? And here's the funniest coincidence of all. There was a fire that day too, wasn't there?"

"Yes," I said. "I think there was, now that I recall it."

"And when you went in, there wasn't anybody in the place, as far as you could see?"

"Yes. That's right."

"But of course you didn't think anything about it? I mean, it happens every day—a bank with money lying around everywhere and nobody in sight looking after it. You didn't think about it again, did you?"

"Yes, I did. As a matter of fact, I thought they were goofier than bedbugs."

"But you went right ahead and put your money in it, didn't you?"

"I had to, if I was going to put it anywhere. It was the only bank in town."

He shifted his attack then. That was the trouble with him; you could never tell where he was going to hit you next. "You're a pretty big man, Madox. How much do you weigh?"

"Around two-fifteen. Why?"

"And just from looking at you I'd say not much of it's fat. There's a lot of power there. What I'm getting at is a long talk I had with Julian Ward. I spent about two hours with him, trying to find something to start with. He didn't see the man who tied him up; all he saw was a blanket. But there was one thing he *was* certain about—and that was whoever did the job was a big man and a powerful one. He said he'd never felt such absolute helplessness in his life."

"Nuts," I said. "I know Ward. He's the man who opened the account for me. He's sixty if he's a day, and he wouldn't weigh 140 in a wet overcoat. A high-school kid could man-handle him."

"Sure. But the thing that stuck in his mind wasn't that it was done, but the *way* it was done. No effort. So much reserve power the man didn't even hurt him, just picked him up and set him down the way you would a baby."

"All right," I said. "So it was a big man. Am I the only one in the state?"

"You're the only one so far that fits exactly in the whole picture."

"Well, look," I said angrily. "Let's get down to some facts. You say the bank was robbed while that building was burned down, that whoever cleaned it out set the building afire so he wouldn't be bothered by kibitzers looking over his shoulder. Well, I was at the fire. So how in hell could I have been in two places at once?"

He stopped and sat down on the edge of the desk again, with what looked like a little smile around the corners of his mouth. "I wondered when you'd get around to that," he said. "Can you prove you were at the fire?"

I had sense enough to lead into it gradually. This white-haired bloodhound could smell a pat alibi a mile. "Well, damn," I said, "somebody must have seen me. After all, there were more than a thousand people milling around——"

"But anybody in particular?" he asked.

"Well, I didn't go around shaking hands and taking down the names and addresses of witnesses, if that's what you mean. But let me think. There's bound to be somebody who remembers me. I talked to some of them——"

"Why not go ahead and say it?" he asked softly. "One of the men you talked to is sitting right there looking at you. He remembers you. He remembers how you made a big splash handling hose and helping shove the crowd back—twenty-five minutes after the fire started, and after the bank was already robbed."

THAT STARTED IT, and it went on and on until time meant
nothing any more. They had Gulick's statement that I'd left
the car lot when the fire engine went by, and they said
nobody had seen me again until a full twenty-five minutes
had gone by. I said I'd been at the fire the whole time. They
said I hadn't. I began to feel dazed, and hypnotized, too
tired to lift my hands or light a cigarette or think. The
world became nothing but heat and white light and an
endless rain of questions beating against me. They took
turns. Tate went out for coffee and when he came back the
Sheriff went out. It made no difference. The questions and
the accusations were the same and after a while I couldn't
tell the voices apart.

"Where did you go that Friday?"

"I went to Houston."

"Where did you go that night?"

"Swimming. I told you. *I went swimming.*"

"You went somewhere to get rid of that money. Where'd
you hide it?"

"I went swimming."

"Did you bury it?"

"I went swimming."

"Where did you bury it?"

"I didn't bury anything."

"How did you mark the place?"

"I went swimming."

"Was it near the river?"

"It was in the river."

"You buried the money in the river?"

"I didn't bury any money. I didn't have any money. I don't know anything about any money."

"Did you bury it along the road somewhere? Did you bury it in a money bag? What kind of bag? What'd you carry it away from the bank in? Did you count it? Don't you know the bank has a record of the serial numbers? You can't spend it. *Where did you hide it?*"

"I didn't bury anything."

"Where did you buy that clock?"

"I never saw the clock before."

"Did you go to Houston?"

"Yes."

"What's the name of the girl?"

"Kelvey."

"I thought Kelvey was the man who owed you money."

"That's what I mean."

"You just said the girl's name was Kelvey. Who owed you money?"

"Kelvey."

"There wasn't any girl, was there? You went down there to buy a clock to make a fire-bomb. *Where'd you buy that clock?*"

"I didn't."

"You stood behind the door in the can and threw a blanket over him when he came in. Why didn't you sap him?"

"I don't know anything about it."

"You knew he was an old man and you were afraid you'd kill him and you didn't want a murder rap on your hands. Wasn't that it?"

"I've told you a thousand times. I was at the fire."

"I'm talking about before you got to the fire."

"I got there within two or three minutes after the fire-truck."

"What time was that?"

"How the hell do I know? Was there *anybody* at the fire who could tell you exactly what time it was?"

"Why didn't somebody see you?"

"They did. Tate saw me."

"Why didn't he see you before the bank was robbed?"

"How do I know? Maybe he did."

"He says he didn't."

"All right. Ask him to name all the other people he saw there, and the exact times he saw them."

"You made a big show when you got there, didn't you? Everybody could see you. But it was too late. That was *after* the bank was robbed."

It went on. I was groggy. After a while I could see yellow light along the wall and thought my mind was becoming unstuck. It was sunlight, coming in through the bars on the window.

They fingerprinted me, took my belt and wallet, and led me upstairs to a cell. I sat down on the side of a bunk with my head in my hands while the whole place revolved slowly around me. I could still hear the questions. The voices wouldn't stop.

Two trusties or turnkeys came down the corridor with breakfast. It consisted of a pile of grey oatmeal on a tin plate and a cup of greenish-black coffee with oil on it. I set the oatmeal on the floor and drank the coffee. It was awful. I had only two cigarettes left, so I tore one in two and smoked half of it.

There was another man in the cell, but I hadn't paid much attention to him until now he came over holding out a cigarette. "If'n you don't want the oatmeal, I'll eat it," he said. "I'll trade you a cigarette for it." He was a thin middle-aged man with sandy hair and a red, sunburned neck like a farmer.

I took it. "Thanks," I said.

I lay down in the bunk and put an arm up over my face to shut out the light and tried to sleep. It wasn't any good. Where did we go from here? I couldn't prove I was at the fire all the time, and they couldn't prove I wasn't. The only thing they had to go on was the fact that that Sheriff knew I was the one who'd done it, knew it absolutely and without doubt—and without any proof at all that they could take into court. Nobody had seen me. They had my fingerprints, but I didn't have a record, and I hadn't left any prints in the bank because I'd used a handkerchief around my hand opening drawers and doors. What did they have on their side? Nothing—except that they could keep on asking questions until I went crazy.

They had to have a confession. And they had to make me show them where the money was so I couldn't repudiate it in court. Could they do it? I didn't know. There wasn't any way to tell what you'd do after two or three days of that.

Sometime in the afternoon they came and got me again. The Sheriff was in the office, along with Buck and Tate, and another man I didn't know. He could have been the prosecuting attorney or one of the detectives from Houston.

"We're going to give you one more chance to come clean," the Sheriff said.

"How much longer does this go on?" I asked.

"Till you tell us what you did with that money."

"I don't know anything about any money."

It was the last session all over again, only worse. Sometimes three of them would be hammering at me at the same time, one in front and one on each side so I'd have to keep turning my head to answer. One would fire a question at me and before I could get my mouth open there'd be two more.

"Where'd you go the night before the fire?"

"How do I know? To the movies, I think."

"Your landlady said she heard you come in around two a.m."

"Where'd you go last night before they picked you up?"

"I told you——"

"Do a lot of running around at night, don't you?"

"In a hell of a hurry to get to that fire, weren't you? Gulick says you took off from there like a ruptured duck. But just why was it *you never did even go near the first one*?"

And then, after about an hour, there was an abrupt change in the attack. Buck left the room, and when he came back he had two more men with him. They were prisoners, because I remembered seeing them upstairs in the cells. He lined the three of us up about four feet apart in a row and then got in the line himself. Tate and the man I didn't know sat in chairs along the other wall, not saying anything and just watching intently. I kept my eye on the Sheriff. He was up to something, and I'd seen enough of him by this time to know it would be dangerous.

"All right, not a word out of any of you," he said, and went over and opened the door. I could feel the tension building up.

"We're ready," he said to somebody in the hall. He stepped outside. I watched the door, conscious of the sweat breaking out on my face. Then he came back, leading someone by the arm. It was the old blind Negro, Uncle Mort.

You could feel the whole room tighten up. The two prisoners were watching the Negro, not knowing what it was all about but scared. I watched him and the Sheriff, feeling all the eyes on me and trying to guess what was coming. The Sheriff led him down the line, stopping him in front of each man about three feet away and facing him.

It was the stillness that made it bad. Nobody said a word. They stood for maybe a minute in front of the first man, and then moved to the next one. It was completely fantastic. It was a police line-up for a blind man.

I was third in line, after the two prisoners. I watched the expressionless black face and the sightless eyes behind the glasses. What was he doing? Listening? Smelling? Or could he actually see? I remembered the way he had tracked me there in the bank. And then I began to get it. It was the silence which tipped me off. He was listening to the breathing of each man when the Sheriff stopped him.

He stopped in front of me. We were facing each other in exactly the same way we had in the bank, and from the same arm's-length distance. It was insane. It would make you scream if you didn't have good nerves. They were trying to prove I had held up the bank, and I was standing right there in the midst of them facing the very man who'd watched me do it—except that he couldn't see. But was there something characteristic about my breathing that would identify me? My nose was broken; was that it? I waited, sweating. He moved on to Buck.

Then they were coming back to me again, and I could see it. They weren't trying to identify my—they were trying to make me break. It was just psychology. A thing like that wouldn't hold up in court, but if they could crack my nerve and make me confess, *that* would. There'd be any one of a hundred signals he could give the Negro to tip him when he was in front of the right man.

They stopped in front of me. The Negro's face was blank as death. "Hit sound like him," he said then.

"You sure, Uncle Mort?" the Sheriff asked.

"Suah sound like him. Got a kind of bleep, like a tea-kettle."

"You've heard it before?"

"Heered it twice befoah. One day about three weeks back, befoah the bank got held up, an' then the next time whilst I'm a-standin' there an' the man holdin' up the bank right in front of me."

"And that first time, there was a fire that day too, wasn't there? And nobody in the bank except this man?"

"Yessuh. That right. I went in to ask Mist' Julian wheahabouts the fiah, only he ain't in theah. Jes' this man. Suah sound like him."

"All right, Uncle Mort. That's all." The Sheriff led him to the door and turned him over to someone in the hall. Buck went out with the two prisoners.

"Sit down, Madox." The Sheriff nodded curtly towards the chair. When I was seated, he said, "All right. You ready to make a statement now? What did you do with the money?"

"So we're back to that again?"

"Why don't you get wise to yourself, Madox? You can see we've got the goods on you. You just trying to make it tougher on yourself?"

"No."

"You heard that Negro. He picked you out of four men. And he can do it in court."

"Not without you there to squeeze his arm."

"I didn't squeeze his arm. He recognized your breathing."

"Bad sweat. What the hell is this, Alice in Wonderland?"

"Have a little trouble getting your breath, don't you, with that broken nose? Ever have a doctor look at it?"

"No."

"Probably don't even notice it yourself, do you? That little whistle, I mean."

"Cut it out, will you? So the man who robbed the bank was breathing."

He stopped directly in front of me and pointed the cigar in my face. "Look, Madox. I'm not trying to find out who robbed that bank. I already know that. *And you know that I know it*. Don't you? So I want to tell you something. You're not going to get away with it. So help me God, I'm going to prove it if it's the last thing I ever do in this world. We'll start at the beginning again. Now tell me where you went when the fire broke out."

I sighed. "Over to the fire, like everybody else in town."

"I mean exactly where were you? In back of the building? In front? Out in the street along the side? Where?"

"In front," I said. "Where the fire-truck was."

"Well, how do you account for the fact that out of over a hundred people I've talked to who were jammed around that fire truck, not one of 'em saw you? I mean, until nearly thirty minutes later, when you made a big show of yourself? Were you hiding behind something?"

"There was a building burning down," I said. "It's just possible they were looking at that."

"All right," he said. "We'll disregard that for the moment. What I want to do right now is clear up a little point that's been bothering me from the first. You were there, you say. Right by the fire-engine all the time. And we know you're a hero, just aching to get in there and help. Tate's already testified to that—how you grabbed the hose and made a grandstand play in front of the whole crowd, after the bank was robbed. Now what I'd like to find out— and the thing that's going to interest the jury—is why you were so bashful about offering to help during the first few minutes, when you really could have done something. *You know what I mean, don't you?* But sure you do. You were there. You admit it yourself."

He paused, with a little smile around his mouth again, looking like a cat getting ready to pounce. I couldn't do anything but wait for it and pray I'd have the answer.

"Now we know you were there. And that you were dying to help. All right." He swung around and pointed the cigar at me and lashed out, "So what was holding you back when that woman became hysterical and started screaming that her little boy was missing and wanted somebody to go in the building and look for him? Why didn't you step up? Were you afraid to go in there? Or you just hadn't made up your mind to be a hero yet? Like hell! I'll tell you why—*it was because you weren't even there, and you know it*. Don't you?"

I opened my mouth. And then I stopped. I could smell it. It was a trap. He'd left the door open too invitingly. But, I thought in an agony of indecision, what if I was wrong? If I said the wrong thing he had me nailed right to the cross. But I had to say something. I took a deep breath and plunged.

"Look," I said. "I was there the whole time, and I didn't even hear any hysterical woman."

I could see it on his face before he wiped it off. I'd guessed it right. But how about the next one, and the one after that, and the one two days from now?

He'd just started to tear into me again when the telephone rang. He walked over and picked it up.

The room was very quiet. "Yes?" he said. "Speaking"—"Where?"—"Oh, sure. Sure"—"You're certain of it?" He was staring at me, frowning. "You're positive of that? And the time?"—"Yes—three blocks, it wouldn't take any longer than that. No, in that case, there couldn't be any doubt of it. All right. Thanks." He hung up.

Suddenly, he looked tired. I waited, almost afraid to breathe. Who was it? What had he said? I wanted to jump up and shake it out of him. He looked at Tate and shook his head wearily, a baffled expression in his eyes.

"That was George Harshaw," he said. "Calling from Galveston. He read about it in the papers. And he says Madox was definitely at the fire the whole time."

Tate was puzzled, too. "Harshaw? I don't remember seeing him there. I think I saw her——"

"That's right. It wasn't George that saw him. It was Mrs. Harshaw. She saw him drive up and get out of his car just as she got there. And it was less than five minutes after the fire broke out."

12

THAT WAS ALL there was to it. They had to let me go. I saw his face as he told Tate to give me a lift back to Lander and it had the expression of a mathematician who'd just seen it proved that two times three is five, but there wasn't anything he could do about it. If Dolores Harshaw had seen me there at the beginning he had no case, and he knew it.

"I'm sorry, Madox," he said stiffly. "There wasn't anything personal about it. I'd have picked up my own brother on the same evidence."

"What the hell," I said. "It's a job, like selling cars. I'll tell you one thing, though. If I ever go into the bank-robbing business, I'll move out of your county."

He stared at me thoughtfully. "Yeah. Do that, will you."

Tate was silent as we drove back to Lander, and I didn't feel like talking either. My mind was too numb to handle anything except the fact that I was free. It was dark by the time we got to town and Tate dropped me off at the rooming house.

I got out. "Thanks," I said. "So long."

"I'll see you." He lifted his hand and drove off.

I wanted to see Gloria Harper. I'd take a shower and change clothes, and then I'd call her. I'd take her to dinner at the restaurant. We'd go riding somewhere. I didn't do any of it. When I got in the shower and the warm water hit me I began to dissolve like a cake of yeast. I hadn't known how bad the pressure really was or how tight I'd been until it started to let go. The reaction unloaded on me, and I just made it into bed before I quit operating.

I awoke sometime before dawn and sat straight up in bed, staring. Who was free? Supposing for a minute that that

Sheriff was naïve enough to buy something that easily, which he wasn't—just what was Dolores Harshaw selling?

I was still his Number One boy as far as he was concerned, and if I dug up the money and tried to leave the country I'd be picked up before I got out of the state. Maybe he'd just pretended to believe her so I'd try it.

And that still left her. What did she want?

After a while I dressed and went downtown. Only a few people were on the street. The waitress did a double take when I came into the restaurant, and I knew a lot of people were going to be surprised to see me around here again. I ordered some breakfast, and stared at the Houston paper without seeing it.

Why had she done it? She'd said she had seen me there at the fire a few minutes after it broke out when she knew damned well she hadn't; she also knew something else none of the rest of them did—that I'd been inside that building and knew what a firetrap it was. Maybe she had some ideas of her own. I gave it up and went out into the street. There was no use knocking myself out worrying about it; I had a hunch I'd be seeing her soon enough.

Gulick was opening the office. He seemed glad to see me.

"Did they find out who did it?" he asked awkwardly.

I went in and sat down on a desk where I could watch the loan office across the street. "No," I said. "I don't think so. They had some kind of pipe dream I was the one until we finally got it straightened out that I was at the fire."

He fidgeted, looking down at his shoes. "I know," he said unhappily. "They were here Saturday, asking about you. I told 'em just what happened as well as I could remember. I hope you don't think I had any idea like that——"

"Of course not," I said. "How was business?"

He looked a little more cheerful. "Good. The paper came out yesterday, with the ad. A lot of people have been in."

"Excuse me," I broke in. "I'll be back in a minute." She was coming along the sidewalk on the other side of the street, very fresh and lovely in the early morning sunlight.

When she saw me crossing towards her she stopped, shy-
ness and confusion and a very warm sort of happiness all
mixed up in her face.

I came up and took her arm. She was still looking up at
me. "Hello," I said.

"Are you all right, Harry?" she asked eagerly. "I mean, is
everything all right? I've been half crazy. Nobody knew
anything, and I couldn't find out anything."

"It's all right now," I said. "It was just a mistake. We got
it straightened out." Somehow, the lies didn't seem to
matter. I wasn't really lying, not about anything between
the two of us. I was just protecting her from something she
had no connection with and which would hurt her if she
knew the truth.

"It was an awful thing for them to do," she said, and
suddenly her eyes were full of anger. I'd never seen her that
way before. "Wait'll I get hold of that Jim Tate. I'll tell him
what I think of him."

"He wouldn't mind," I said. "Not if he could look at you
while you're telling him."

"Well, I'd tell him anyway," she said defiantly, and then
all the vehemence went out of her and she was just con-
fused and happy. "You're teasing me."

"No," I said. "I'm not teasing you." That terrific aware-
ness of her began to get the best of me, and I wanted to
take hold of her and kiss her so badly my arms hurt. She
must have seen it in my face.

"Harry, I have to get to work!" she said hurriedly.

I walked with her up to the door. She unlocked it, and
paused a moment in the doorway. "Sometime in the next
year or so it'll be five o'clock," I said. "I'll see you then."

She smiled. "I think it could be arranged."

Somehow the day wore on. The hours dragged, but never
did come to a complete standstill. We were busy, which
helped a little. About three o'clock I drove back on to the
lot after a short ride with a farmer who wanted a demon-
stration, and saw her come out of the office across the street
and start up the sidewalk. I stopped in the middle of my
sales pitch when I saw who was with her. It was Sutton.

The farmer hemmed and hawed and reckoned he'd have to think it over a little more. "Sure," I said impatiently. "O.K. O.K." I could still see them. They were turning in at the drugstore. He finally shuffled off and I slammed the car door shut and started walking across the street after them.

They were sitting in a booth. She was facing the front, and as I came through the door I got a glimpse of her face before she saw me. It was unhappy and afraid and somehow defenceless, as if she had come to expect humiliation from Sutton and knew of no way to escape it. There was something beaten about it. When she looked up and saw me I could see her begging me to stay away.

I was in no mood to pay any attention to it. There was nothing in my mind now except Sutton. I pulled up a chair and sat down at the end of the table, glancing at her and then at him.

"Well," I said, "a little business meeting?"

He nodded affably, and then he said, "Sure. Why don't you sit down? Oh, I see you already have."

"You don't mind, do you?" I asked.

"Not at all."

I leaned my arms on the table and looked at him. "You're sure it's all right? With you, I mean. You don't have any objections?"

"Not a one, pal."

"Well, that's nice," I said. "Isn't it?" But I knew it wasn't any use. Crowding him like that was just a waste of time. He was too much of the pro. He was pushing her around for what he could get out of it, and being jockeyed into a useless fight was only for suckers.

"Anything I could help with?" I asked.

"No-o, I don't think so," he said. Then he looked across at her and asked, with bland innocence, "Do you think there's anything he could help with, honey?"

Her face was pale and you could see her fighting to keep from going all to pieces. I began to wonder if I was being very smart. I was blundering around in something I didn't know anything about, and I began to have a feeling it was too deep to be cleared up by a kid stunt like slapping Sutton around, even if I could do it. She could only shake her head.

"Well, I'm sorry, pal," he said with mock regret. "You see how it is. Maybe some other time, huh? We'll give you a ring."

"Please, Harry," she said miserably, "it's all right. It's just a personal matter I have to talk over with Mr. Sutton."

"O.K.," I said. I shook my head and got up. There wasn't anything else to do. I looked down at Sutton. "Sorry we couldn't do any business."

"Well, cheer up, pal. There's days like that," he said easily. "I'd cry, but it makes my mascara run."

I went back to the lot. If she wouldn't tell me what it was and didn't want me mixed up in it, there was nothing I could do. I groused around the lot the rest of the afternoon. I already had an idea what it would be like when I picked her up at five o'clock, and it was. It was ruined. She was completely different when she had seen Sutton, or even when I mentioned him. She was tightened up and silent, and you could sense the desperate unhappiness tearing her up inside. We stopped on a little country road and I kissed her, but it wasn't anything. She was somewhere else.

"I'm sorry," she said miserably. "I hate to be such a wet blanket, Harry. And I was looking forward so to seeing you."

I took her face in my hands as I had that night. "Come on," I said. "Let's have it."

She just shook her head with an infinite weariness.

"Don't you see?" I said. "You've got to tell me. How can I help you if I don't know what it is?"

"There's nothing you can do, Harry."

"The hell there's not. It's Sutton, isn't it?"

She didn't answer for a moment, and then she nodded slowly.

"Well, Sutton puts his pants on one leg at a time, just like everybody else. All he needs is for somebody to have a talk with him."

"No," she said desperately. "Don't do it, Harry! Promise me you'll stay away from him."

"Why?"

"Because. You have to. You just have to," she said pleadingly. "Just give me a little time. Don't you see? It isn't that I don't want to tell you. I just can't—not yet. It's all so mixed up. I almost go crazy trying to decide what to do. It was bad enough before, but now——"

"But now what?" I asked, turning her face so she had to look at me.

"Now there's you," she said simply.

I kissed her and sat there holding her with the top of the blonde head just under my chin. Her face was pressed into my shirt and she was crying, quite silently. I thought of Sutton. If we had much more of this, something was going to happen to him.

We went to the movies Wednesday night, and she began to snap out of it a little. Neither of us had seen anything more of Sutton. She was very quiet, but she didn't break down any more, and I just gave her time as she had asked me. I knew she was fighting it out with herself, and once or twice I had the feeling she was very near to telling me about it. She never did quite make it, but I left her alone. I knew that was what she wanted, and it was wonderful just being with her.

Gulick and I were busy at the lot, with the cars moving pretty well, and I was starting to work up another ad. I thought about the buried money a hundred times a day, but stayed away from the place. The uproar over the robbery was dying down a little, but I knew now I was being watched. The whole thing telegraphed itself. They'd given up too easily when they got that phone call from Harshaw. The alibi she'd handed me was second-hand and hearsay, coming to them through Harshaw, and yet they'd just folded up and quit as if she'd already testified to it under oath. I wasn't free; I was just being allowed to run around on the end of a line until I hanged myself. Well, it was all right; two could play at that game. As long as I left the money where it was, I was safe. They had nothing else to go on, and they'd never find it.

Gulick and I were sitting in the office around four o'clock Thursday afternoon when the phone rang. He answered.

"Hello," he said. "Harshaw's Car Lot. Hello! Hello!" Then he put the receiver back in the cradle.

"Wrong number?" I asked.

"I don't know," he said. "They just hung up."

About twenty minutes later the same thing happened again. I began to have a feeling about it then. The third time it rang he was outside and I answered myself. My hunch was right.

"It's about time you answered," she said. Her voice was pitched very low and I had a little trouble hearing it.

"We didn't expect you back so soon," I said, giving it the employee-to-boss's-wife treatment. "I hope you had a nice trip."

"Aren't you cute?" she said. "Cut it out."

"I didn't think you'd be back till Monday."

"I'll tell you about that. When I see you. Tonight, that is."

I looked up just then and saw Gulick coming back in from the lot. "Well, I don't know." I said. "It depends on how much you want for it. That model's three years old."

She was fast enough on the uptake. "Oh," she said, "So old prissy-pants is there?"

"Yes," I said. "That's right."

"Well, he can't hear me. So listen. Go to the same place you went before——"

Gulick sat down and started reading the paper at the next desk. "I don't think we can made any deal on that basis," I said.

"Don't you really?" she asked softly. Something in her voice told me she was enjoying it.

"No."

"Well, that *is* too bad, isn't it?" she purred. Then she went on, "Oh, by the way, wasn't it lucky I saw you over there the other day at the fire? Just suppose I'd missed you."

"Yes, that's right," I said. I could feel the snare begin to tighten around my neck. It was nylon and very smooth, and all she was doing was adjusting my tie for me, the dirty little...

"I did so want to see you," she said regretfully. "But of course, if you've got another date——"

"I'll tell you what," I said. "I'll think it over."

"You're so nice. The same time as before, then?"

"Yes."

"All right. 'Bye now."

I was furious as I drove out the highway after dark, but I was scared too. If it had been dangerous before, it was suicidal now. There wasn't only Harshaw and the gossips to think about; there was that Sheriff. She had furnished me with an alibi, so how long would it take him to get suspicious if he even heard of our being seen together? And what were they doing back here on Thursday, four days ahead of time? It was funny, too, that he hadn't come to the office. The whole thing was crazy.

Just before I turned off at the old gravel pit I checked the road behind me. There some other headlights, two or three sets of them, about a half mile back. I made my turn anyway, and drove on into the timber. All the cars went on past without slowing down. I still wasn't sure, though, and I felt uneasy.

I drove along the road until I found what I was looking for, a place where I could pull off into the trees and get the car out of sight. After I got it turned around facing the road again I cut the lights and waited. I'd have a pretty good look at anyone going past, but there'd be no chance he'd see me back of that screen of leaves and underbrush.

I lighted a cigarette and smoked it out nervously, listening to the night sounds and thinking of the dangerous mess I was drifting further into all the time. I had twelve thousand dollars I couldn't touch, I was crazy about a girl who was in some kind of trouble she couldn't tell me about, and I was getting more hopelessly fouled up every day with this crazy Dolores Harshaw. I had to ditch her while I was still able to.

13

MINUTES DRAGGED BY, I finished the cigarette and crushed it out in the tray. Then I heard a car coming and could see splashes of light breaking against the trees. It came up past me and went on. I had a fairly good look at it and was sure it was the Oldsmobile. But maybe I'd better wait a few minutes and be sure she wasn't being followed. Then I had a better idea; it couldn't be over a quarter mile to the old sawmill, so why not walk? If I heard another car coming I could jump out of the road and take to the timber.

There wasn't any other car. My eyes became accustomed to the sooty blackness under the trees, and when I came out into the clearing around the old mill I could see fairly well in the starlight. The Olds was parked off the road at the edge of the clearing. She wasn't in it. Then I spotted her, a gleam of white over by the old sawdust pile. She was stand-ing near the back of it, where it slid off into the shadowy depths of the ravine.

When I came up I saw why she'd been so easy to see. She was wearing only a pair of brief, pale-coloured shorts and a halter, and all that stacked and uncovered blondeness was almost luminous in the darkness.

She turned when she heard me, and put her arms up. They tightened around my neck as she came up against me. You could no more halfway kiss her than you could fall part way down an elevator shaft and then change your mind, but even so she knew something was wrong.

"What's the matter?" she asked. "Don't tell me I'm slipping?"

I drew back a little. "What'd you have to see me about?"

"Now I've heard everything."

The anger came boiling up in me again. Maybe she thought she owned me. "Well, if that's all," I said, "let's get on with it. If we hurry, maybe we can make the next train home."

Her palm exploded against my face and made my eyes sting. I grabbed her arm and tightened up on it. "Keep your hand to yourself, you little witch," I said, "or I'll break it off."

"Well, so we've got another girl now, have we?"

"And whose business would that be if I had?"

"It might be mine. You ever think of that?"

"It's not. And I didn't."

"You might be surprised." She looked up at me with a tantalizing smile. "Now, let's see. It wouldn't be that leggy blonde in the loan office, would it? What's her name? Harper? I saw you at the movies with her. But no, I guess she's not quite your type. Pretty, all right, but a little young and watered-down for you."

"Knock it off," I said. "If you wanted to see me about something, start talking."

"So it *is* the little dear?" She laughed. "Well, how do you like that? She must be the sly one, all right, with that innocent look. But I guess you can never tell about that long-underwear type.'

I caught myself just in time. I couldn't let her needle me into losing my head. There was something a little too cocky about her which got home to me, even through the blaze of anger, and I had to find out what she was up to.

"Let's get down to cases," I said. "I came out here to tell you something. Don't call me up any more. I don't like it. And this is the last time I'm going to meet you out here. You may be crazy, but I'm not. If you've got to play in the sawdust to keep yourself from jumping at night, go find yourself another boy friend. I'm through."

"My goodness," she said. "You *are* in a state tonight, aren't you? What's she been doing to you, taking you to church? Or maybe you're still a little nervous?"

"What do you mean by that?"

"It must have been just *awful*. Imagine them thinking you did it."

I could feel it coming, but went on playing it deadpan. "Well, I guess they had to pick up somebody. But what's that got to do with it?"

"Well, nothing, I suppose," she said innocently. "Except that—— Well, I suppose I thought you'd be glad to see me. After all, I did see you there, and I was the only one, wasn't I?"

"Probably others did, and just didn't remember," I said, beginning to sweat. "The fact that you saw me proves I was there, so there must have been more."

"But it was so stupid of them not to remember, wasn't it?"

"Well, maybe they just didn't know me."

"At least, not as well as I do."

"I can't see that it matters now, anyway," I said. "After all, somebody saw me there, and that settles it. But don't think I'm not glad you did. It was a break for me."

"Oh, it was for me too," she said earnestly. "Just for the sweet things you said. Remember?"

"Oh, sure," I said.

"I knew you would. It was right at the beginning. I was watching the fire-engine hook on to the water line, and you came over to where I was standing and said you'd never seen me looking prettier and that you wished we were alone. You remember that, don't you?"

The dirty, rotten little... "Yes," I said. "And what else did I say?"

"Why, let me see now. You said it was funny it was that building, because we'd just been in it the other day, and who'd have thought all those old papers and trash and junk would catch fire like that? Of course, nobody else knew that——"

"I see," I said. "It was quite a conversation, wasn't it. Was that all?"

"Well, not quite. You said nobody could ever take my place, and you'd never be able to leave me. I thought that was awful sweet. Don't you?"

"Yes," I said. "Very sweet. So now let's cut it out. What's the angle?"

"Why, nothing at all, sweet. Except that I'd hate to think you didn't mean all those nice things you said to me."

"And if I told you to go to hell?"

"Then I'd know I just dreamed the whole thing. Wouldn't that be awful?"

She knew she didn't have to say the rest of it. Without her alibi I'd be headed right back to the quiz show and maybe this time they'd break me. She had me right where she wanted me.

"I love talking to you," she said, smiling. "We understand each other so well. You know, in a lot of ways we're just alike."

"Isn't that nice?" I said.

"Yes, I think so. Now kiss me like a good boy, and tell me you like me better than that skinny little owl."

There was no way to kiss her like a good boy. You could start out that way, but you always ended up on the other side of the tracks. If you hated her, it didn't make any difference; it worked just the same.

"M-m-m!" she said. "See? You do like me, don't you?"

"No."

"Isn't that funny? I could have sworn you did. But, honey, before you get carried away with not liking me, I just remembered there was something I wanted to tell you."

"What's that?"

"This will kill you. I think I got caught one of those other times."

She had me in such a cross-fire by now I couldn't even think. I just looked at her stupidly. "You got what?"

"Caught. You know. As in caught. I think I'm pregnant."

"Well, why tell me? After all, you're married."

"I just thought you might be interested."

"What are you going to do?"

"Look," she said. "I'll show you."

At first I thought she had gone crazy, and then I was sure of it. She was just staring down into the ravine. The place we were standing was a little to one side of the sawdust pile, on the brink of the ravine itself. The sawdust was stacked up maybe as high as a two-storey house, and as the pile had grown and spread while the mill was operating, it had edged further out all the time until the back edge of it spilled over the bank. It was very steep and probably fifty or seventy-five feet to the bottom. You couldn't be sure, however. It was very dark down there in the trees and you couldn't see the bottom.

But it was what she did next that got me. She just jumped, without any warning at all, right out on to the steep slope of the sawdust. An avalanche of the stuff carried away and went down with her as she rolled and slid out of sight into the dense shadow below me. I stared down, completely speechless with amazement.

She's a psycho, I thought. She's completely off her trolley. One minute she's a blackmailer as cagey as Kruschev, and the next she wants to gambol half-naked on a pile of sawdust like a babe on an absinthe jag. It made me cold to think about it. This was the oversexed and rudderless maniac who could throw me back to the cops any time.

I looked down and I could see the white gleam of her in the edge of the shadows. She was trying to come back up, and she was doing it the hard way. Instead of going down the ravine to a place she could walk out, she was trying to climb right up that steep incline of loose sawdust. She was sinking in it halfway up her thighs, like a man walking in deep snow, and every few feet she'd start a new avalanche and lose the little she'd gained. It was man-killing work. She fought it with a fury I didn't know she had in her. Every time she'd slide back she'd tear into it again, lifting her legs high and battling it. It would have killed anyone with a bad heart. I watched her fight her way up the last few feet and then collapse exhausted on the edge of the slope. The laboured sound of her breathing seemed to fill the night.

"Well!" She stopped and took a long, shaky breath. "How was that?"

"All right, I guess, if you enjoyed it."

"Enjoyed it? Are *you* silly!"

"Well, what'd you do it for?"

"Don't be stupid, darling. I just told you."

Suddenly the light burst on me. She hadn't blown her top at all. The whole thing had been quite sane and deadly. "You mean, just throwing yourself down the hill like that——?"

She laughed then. "No, dear. Not falling down the hill. Climbing back up."

"Are you sure?"

'It always works for me. I'm lucky that way."

It began to come home to me then that maybe I didn't know all there was to know about her. I began to sense a steel-trap deadliness of purpose operating somewhere behind that baby stare and sensuous face. She was as tough as a shark, and she got what she wanted. She'd be hard to whip, because she got fat on her enemies. She got in trouble on a sawdust pile, so she used the sawdust pile to cure it.

She motioned to me to squat down beside her. "Light me a cigarette, Harry?" she said.

I got one out, and in the brief, yellow flare of the match she looked up at me with eyes that were almost black. Her face and body were shiny with sweat, and sawdust was sticking to her and to her clothes.

She glanced down at herself. "Damn," she said. "I should have taken them off, shouldn't I?"

She reached coolly around behind her and unsnapped the halter and slipped out of it. She shook it, and then brushed carelessly at the sawdust on her breasts. I was still holding the cigarette and the match. She looked up at my face and smiled at what she saw there, then reached out and took the cigarette from me. The match burned down and scorched the ends of my fingers. I cursed, my voice sounding strange and almost unrecognizable.

"Poor old Harry," she said tantalizingly, out of the sudden darkness. "He doesn't like me."

"You lousy little witch," I said, trying to talk past the choking tightness in my throat. "What's it got to do with liking you?"

"I told you we were a lot alike, didn't I?"

"Yes. And don't do it again."

I saw the red trail of the cigarette as she threw it out into the darkness of the ravine. She took hold of my hand and placed it against her cheek. "Lean down, Harry. You want to kiss me, don't you?"

I leaned down. I couldn't help it. There was a roaring like a big river inside my head. I shifted the hand down to her throat. "I'll kill you," I said. "So help me, I'll kill you."

"No, you won't," she said softly. "Not now. Just kiss me now."

Her arms went up around my neck and tightened. And then we were slipping over the edge. Another big slide of sawdust gave way and we were half-buried in it, locked together and tumbling, sliding, rolling over and over all the way to the bottom. We came to rest somewhere at last and the world stopped whirling and settled into place. Her arms were still tight around me and her lips were against my ear. They were moving, and the whisper was ragged and frantic, and then incoherent in its urgency. It was very dark there in the ravine under the trees. It was just as well.

"And you thought you could leave me."

I lay there, hating her, not touching her but knowing how near she was in the darkness. I didn't say anything.

"You and that prissy little owl. That Sunday-school kid. You think you could leave me for her?"

"I told you. I'm through. This is the last time."

"That's what you think.

"About us. We belong together. If you left me, you'd come back. What's the use of trying to kid yourself? We're just two people who take what we want, and we belong together. We need each other. You said I was a tramp; well, did you ever stop to think you're one too?"

"So you admit it? Why'd you throw an ice-cube tray at me that night?"

"I'm just touchy when I'm drunk. I don't know why. I always suspect everybody of thinking I'm a bitch. And when I'm sober I couldn't care less."

"Well, that's a break."

"Why?"

"Is there anybody who thinks you're not one?"

"You couldn't prove it by me. But I do all right. So do you. I know what I want, and I get it."

"Well, let's get something straight. You think I'm going to marry you? Haven't you forgotten something?"

"What's that?"

"Well, there are actually several things. One is that I wouldn't marry you on a bet. I've already been married to one big-hearted girl who couldn't remember where she lived, and once around the course is enough for any man. But the big thing I had in mind is that you've already got a husband. Remember? Or do you, very often?"

"Probably as often as you do. But never mind about him. He got everything he paid for."

"What do you mean?"

"Do you know why we came back from Galveston today?"

I'd forgotten about that. "No. How could I?"

"He had a heart attack."

"What!"

"It was the second one."

"Where is he now?"

"At home. He wouldn't stay in the hospital."

"When was it?"

"Let's see. It was Monday afternoon I got him to call the Sheriff up here, wasn't it? So it was Tuesday morning."

"How did it happen?"

"He was fighting a big shark, trying to keep it from get-ing the line around the anchor or something, and swearing at the boatman at the same time, and he just fell over. We brought him in to the hospital. He almost didn't make it."

"What did the doctors say?" I knew I was in a funny position to be feeling concerned for him, but I did.

"If he has another one, it may kill him."

"Why wouldn't he stay in the hospital?"

"He hates 'em. And he never pays any attention to doctors. But they warned him he'd better this time. He has to cut out that fishing, and the cigars. And not do any work for several months, and only a little then. Nothing that will excite him. You know what that means?"

"Sure. Just what you said. No more big-game fishing. No more blowing his top over business and government forms and taxes."

"It means more than that. Remember, I told you he'd had two? Well, he wasn't fighting a shark when he had the first one."

14

I WAS DEAD the next day; it was worse than a hangover. Even after I'd gone home I couldn't sleep. I kept thinking of her and what she could do to me, and for some reason I couldn't get Harshaw out of my mind. It didn't make much sense. Why should I worry about him? But every time I'd close my eyes and try to sleep the whole thing would start around again, his lying there alone in the dark listening to it like a mechanic to a missing engine and knowing that when it started to go away again he was done because there wasn't anybody to do anything or even to be there when he left, while all the time the two of us were out there wallowing in our own cheapness. It was a little hard to sleep with.

I was so filled with disgust I didn't even go across the street to see Gloria. I didn't know whether I could face her. The news was out, and everybody was talking about Harshaw's heart attack.

The following day I began to feel a little better. It was Saturday, and we were pretty busy. Around noon the telephone rang.

"Mr. Madox?"

What now? I thought. "Yes. Speaking."

"This is Mrs. Harshaw. George asked me to call you. He isn't feeling well enough to come down to the office, you know. I guess you've heard about it——?" She let it trail off.

"Yes," I said. "I hated to hear it. How is he now?"

"He's a little better. That's the reason I'm calling. He'd like to have you come out to the house tonight to talk over some business details. Do you think you could make it, around seven o'clock?"

"Sure," I said.

"That'll be fine, then. And would you mind telling the girl in the loan office, Miss—ah——"

"Harper," I said. The lousy tramp. She just couldn't resist it.

"Yes. That's it. Miss Harper. He wants her to come too."

"All right," I said. "I'll tell her."

I went across the street. She was busy with a Negro who was making a payment on his loan. When she saw me waiting she waved the pencil at me and her eyes crinkled up in a smile. In a minute the Negro said, "Thank you, Miss Gloria," and went out.

"Hello," she said.

"You're looking very pretty." I paused. We were both always just a little awkward with each other when we first met.

"Do you like my new dress?"

I looked at it. It was blue with white sort of ruffles. "Yes," I said. "Very much."

She smiled. "It isn't new. You've seen it four times."

I shook my head. "I've never seen it at all."

"You're nice." Then her face became serious and she said quietly, "It's so awful about Mr. Harshaw, isn't it?"

"Yes. But I just talked to Mrs. Harshaw, and I think he's a little better. He wants us to come out there tonight. Something about the business. If you can make it, I'll pick you up a little before seven."

"All right, Harry. But he shouldn't be trying to think about business now. What do you suppose he wants?"

"Probably just a report," I said. "But there's no telling. Maybe he's going to sell out and retire."

She didn't answer for a minute. Then she asked, "Do you really think he will?"

Something in her voice made me turn and look at her. It still puzzled me after I left. She had seemed almost afraid. But why should she be? Even if she lost her job, which was unlikely, there were plenty of others.

It was dusk when I drove over to pick her up. She wasn't quite ready, and I waited, talking about cars with the

Robinsons on the front porch. When she came out she was very lovely in a white skirt and dark, long-sleeved blouse, and as we went down the walk and I helped her into the car I was conscious of a faint fragrance about her in the air.

The street going up past the filling station was deserted in the twilight, and just as we came to the oaks I stopped the car.

"Did you forget something, Harry?" she asked.

"No," I said. "I didn't forget it. This is just the first chance I've had to do it." I took her face in my hands and kissed her.

When her eyes opened they smiled at me. There was just enough light to see them. They were enormous. "You mustn't get lipstick on you. We're going to a business conference."

"The devil with business conferences. I just wanted to tell you something. Maybe I never told you before. You're lovely; and you're wonderful."

"Now you're making me lose interest in business."

"I'll tell you what," I said. "We'll sneak out right after we've voted our stock."

She laughed. And then, as I started the car again, she said soberly, "I do hope he's better, Harry. It's so awful thinking of him that way."

He was sitting up in a big chair in the living room, wearing pyjamas and a seersucker robe. He looked old somehow. His face was a dirty grey and seemed thinner, though that might have been just imagination. The only things unchanged about him were the eyes. They were as frosty and tough as ever, and you somehow got the impression that his heart might kill him but it'd never scare him worth a damn.

She let us in. She was wearing a white summer dress and every ash-blonde curl was in place. Her face was heavily made up, but it didn't quite cover up the faint shadows under the eyes. Climbing that sawdust pile was rough medicine, but apparently it'd worked. She was a tough baby. I saw her giving Gloria the inventory. No doubt she'd seen her before, but now she was putting her through the assay office a piece at a time. There was a thirty-looking-at-twenty-one appraisal in her eyes and she didn't quite cover up all the hardness in them.

"You know Miss Harper, don't you? And Madox?" he asked her. I was surprised at his voice. It was a little shaky, and it had lost most of that parade-ground bark.

"Oh, yes, of course. Won't you sit down?" And then she murmured to Gloria, "That's a lovely blouse. I like it."

She excused herself after a fill-in on how he was feeling and said she'd go out in the kitchen and fix some drinks. When she was gone, Harshaw asked, "How's it going?"

"Pretty good," I said. I told him how many cars we'd sold and about a couple we'd taken in on trades.

"You think the ad did any good?"

"Sure. I've got another one in this week's paper."

He grunted. "O.K. I'll tell you what I asked you over here for, but before I do, how'd you get crossed up with that Sheriff?"

I shrugged. "I don't know. For one thing, I was new here. And according to that cashier the robber was a big man."

"It's lucky for you Dolly saw you over there at the fire. I know that bird. In two days he can make you believe you're guilty yourself." He stopped to take a deep breath. He didn't have much strength. "But never mind that. Here's what I've got in mind——"

Just then she came out of the dining room and interrupted him. "It's those darn ice-cube trays, George. They're stuck again. Maybe Mr. Madox——"

"Sure," I said, getting up. "Excuse me."

The little witch, I thought; when she wants to throw 'em at somebody they're not stuck. I followed her through the dining room and out into the kitchen. She watched me as I opened the refrigerator and took the trays out.

"That's funny," she said, smiling. "I couldn't budge 'em."

"Anything else?" I asked.

"Well, you could put the cubes in the glasses if you'd like."

I put them in four glasses. She poured whisky and soda in three of them and plain soda in the fourth. Then she began stirring, making a lot of noise. With the other hand she caught my lapel, and jerked her head for me to come nearer.

She looked up at me, still with that hard smile on her mouth. "Very pretty, isn't she?" she asked, not whispering, but keeping her voice low. Her nostrils dilated a little as she sniffed. "And you can tell the angel-faced little bitch to quit leaving her tracks on you. I can smell her all over you."

"You're crowding your luck," I said. "Don't go too far."

"Maybe you thought I was joking. You'd better keep it in mind."

"I've told you once," I said. "Don't threaten me." I caught the arm that was stirring, pried the spoon out of her fingers, and threw it on the drainboard. "Shall we take the drinks in?"

We went in and passed the drinks around and sat down. Gloria glanced at me with her eyes shining.

"Madox, I've just been telling Miss Harper," he said. "Here's the deal. I'm going to have to quit trying to work, at least for a long time. So I want you to take charge of everything down there. She'll continue to run the loan office, just as she has been, but you'll be responsible for the whole works. I'll pay you a salary, plus your own commissions and the sales-manager's take on what Gulick sells. You ought to be good for around six thousand a year. Do you want it?"

Did I? I thought. It was a terrific break, and it took me a little by surprise. I didn't understand it. We'd always fought like a couple of sore-headed bears. "Sure," I said, trying to get my breath. "Of course I do. But why me? I mean, Gulick's the senior man——"

He gestured curtly. There was still a little of the old Harshaw there. "Gulick can't handle it," he grunted. "He hasn't got the drive. I know you have, and you're too disagreeable to be crooked, so it's yours if you want it."

Sure, I thought. I'm not crooked. Besides betraying him with his wife, all I've done lately is steal twelve thousand dollars. It was a little hard to look at him.

It didn't take long to straighten out the details. Just before we left she had to go with Gloria to show her where the bathroom was, and as they went out of the room he looked after them. It was the first time I'd ever seen anything gentle in his face. I wondered which one he was looking at.

"That's one of the finest girls who ever lived," he said. And then I knew. He was speaking of Gloria. "You won't have to pull any of your hardboiled stuff on her. So don't, or you won't be there."

As soon as we were out in the car she said simply, "I'm so happy for you, Harry. I think it's wonderful."

I turned south on Main Street and drove down the highway. Without conscious thought I made the turn on to the road going up past the abandoned farmhouses. We were both silent now, as the road wound into the river bottom. It was black here in the timber. In a few minutes we came to the river. I stopped the car off the road at the end of the bridge and turned off the lights. The night closed in around us. I got out and went around the car to her door and opened it and helped her out.

When my eyes became accustomed to the darkness I could see the river, the stars reflected on the surface like silver dust across a mirror, and the ghostly outline of the bridge. We walked out on to it, her high heels rapping on the planks. We stopped and stood at the railing, looking down into the blackness and the water. I turned and I could see her face in the faint light here in the open between the walls of trees. The eyes were dark, looking quietly up at me, and there was just a whisper of that fragrance about her. I reached out and put my arms around her.

For a long time there were no words. I was kissing her and then holding her, like something very precious that might fly away, holding her with my face down against her cheek. Then she stirred a little and moved back and as my arms relaxed she took both of my hands and lifted them up against her face.

"The way you did before," she said softly. "It's crazy, isn't it, but I love for you to kiss me that way. Maybe it's because that was the way it was the first time you kissed me. Do you remember that, Harry?"

"No," I said. "I've forgotten it entirely. It was just a little thing, like having a house fall on you." I held her face that way and bent down until I was just touching her lips. "I love you," I said.

"I love you, too, Harry."

"You do?"

"Yes. It's kind of funny. I've known you only about a month, but I can't seem to remember what it was like when I wasn't in love with you. I guess I ought to die of shame for telling you, but you'll never know how much I was hoping you'd kiss me that night when you brought Spunky home."

"You're a crazy kid," I said. "And wonderful."

We were silent again, and after a while she asked softly, "What are you thinking about?"

"I was just wondering how we happened to come to this place. I think I knew right from the minute we left Harshaw's that I was going to ask you if you'd marry me, and I just drove out here without even thinking about it. And I was remembering something he said when you were out of the room."

"What was that, Harry?"

"It's a little funny now. He said he'd fire me if I didn't treat you right. On the job, he meant. You know he's pretty crazy about you, too. He said you were the finest girl he'd ever seen."

"Don't say that, Harry!" She tightened up suddenly in my arms, and I could hear the beginnings of panic in her voice. "Don't say anything. Just hold me."

I held her, but it wasn't any good. I could feel her going to pieces. And then she was crying, not silently as she had before but with a shaken hopelessness that tore me up. There wasn't anything I could do until she quietened. It was an awful feeling.

It was a long time. When she was still at last I took out my handkerchief and mopped away the tears, and then I got hold of her arm and led her back to the car. We got in and I lighted a cigarette and held it for her while she puffed at it.

"All right," I said, "start at the beginning. We've got all night, and we're not going to leave here till you tell me. Something's hurting you, and it's gone far enough. So let's have it."

"All right, I'll tell you, Harry," she said dully. "I can't stand it any more. I've got to tell you. And I'll have to tell him, too. That's the awful part of it. After the way he's treated me, how can I tell—Harry, how can I?"

"Tell who?" I asked.

"Mr. Harshaw." Her voice began to tighten up again. "I've been stealing from him, Harry. I've stolen nearly two thousand dollars from him." It caught up with her again.

It's fine, I thought. It's wonderful. Harshaw should write a book about his faith in the human race. His wife's a tramp, I've been helping her with it, and now this. And then I knew it didn't fit. Two of us were guilty, but Gloria didn't belong in the crowd.

There was nothing to do until she recovered, and then I said gently, "All right, baby. You just tell me what it is. We'll straighten it out. There are two of us now." I lighted her another cigarette and pulled her back to where she could rest her head against my arm.

"I'm sorry, Harry. But I think I'm all right now. I don't think I can make you understand why I did it, because you're not the kind of coward I was, but I'll tell you the best I can. It's been going on for nearly a year now. I keep paying the money back, but I can't catch up with it because of the interest——"

She's unique, I thought. She tells me she's a thief, but still she's paying interest on the money she stole.

"I won't try to tell you what it's like," she went on quietly, with that hopelessness in her voice. "Just trying to keep going, I mean, trying to keep the books straight, paying back a few dollars here and a few there, and then having to write out another fake note to cover one that has to be paid. It all comes to over fifteen hundred dollars, and the interest on it takes up nearly half of what I can pay back out of my salary each month. And then there's always more. Something new. Another twenty or thirty or fifty dollars. But I guess I'd better tell you where it all went, where it goes——"

"That I already know, honey," I said. "What I want to find out before I go to talk to him is *why*."

She shook her head with frantic entreaty. "No, Harry. No! Don't you see that's one reason I haven't told you before? I mean, for fear of what you'd do. He might hurt you, or you might get into trouble over it."

"You can tell me, baby," I said. "And don't worry about it. We'll just have a little talk. It's just possible I speak his language a little better than you do."

She hesitated a minute and then she said unhappily, "All right. But there isn't anything we can do. Except to go and tell him. Mr. Harshaw, I mean. Once I can get up the courage to do that ... but I might as well start at the beginning. It's about a girl, or a woman rather, who came here about this time last year. Her name was Irene Davey. She was a teacher. She'd been hired to teach high-school maths —algebra and plane geometry, I think—and to coach the girls' basketball team. School didn't start until September, of course, but she came along late in August to find a place to live. I met her on the tennis court one day just after she came.

"She was several years older than I was—I guess she was twenty-six or twenty-eight—but she was very good at sports. She was crazy about all kinds of games. She could always beat me at tennis without even trying, and kept asking me about places to swim around here. I understood she had been on the swimming team in college, and had won a number of diving competitions. She seemed to take a great liking to me right from the first. She called me a couple of times and asked me to go to the show with her. I introduced her to a few boys I knew, but she didn't seem to be much interested in them."

She stopped, and then she said, "This is a lot of explanation, Harry, but I have to tell you all of this before you'll understand what happened. It was awful. But I didn't know——"

No, I thought, she probably didn't. I was beginning to have an odd feeling about it, a kind of premonition. What I was remembering was the scene that Sunday morning when they had me trapped up there in that old barn.

15

She went on. "Anyway, Miss Davey came by the house one Saturday afternoon when I was home alone and wanted to go swimming. I told her I didn't like the idea of swimming in the river because it had snags in it and there might be snakes, but she seemed so anxious to try it I finally gave in. I put my bathing suit on, with slacks over it, left a note telling my Sister where I'd gone, and we started down here. We went in her car. I thought about this place because I remembered there was a pool just below the bridge.

"When we got here it was still early in the afternoon and the sun was awfully hot. We took off the clothes we had on over our swim-suits, but she didn't seem to be nearly as eager to swim as she had been. She wanted to talk. We sat in the car and smoked a cigarette, almost in this same spot we're in now, and she told me how much she appreciated my being so nice to her and that she liked me very much. It was a little embarrassing, but I just thought she was lonely and eager to make friends here and I didn't want to be too stand-offish and rude and hurt her feelings. But then she started telling me I was very pretty, and how I looked in a bathing suit——"

She broke off then. I could feel her shudder slightly. "It's awfully hard to tell you this, Harry," she said hesitantly.

"It's all right, honey," I said. "You can skip most of it if you want to. There's nothing new about it, and I can guess the rest."

"I'm glad you understand," she said. "I—I guess I was awfully naïve. I was just uncomfortable and wanted to get out of the car because some of the things she was saying were so personal. And then—— It was horrible. She was trying to kiss me. I was so absolutely frozen with terror I couldn't do anything at first, and then I tried to get out. She was talking to me and trying to hold me back, and I began to fight at her. She was terribly strong. I was crying by this time and trying to get the door open and push her away all at the same time when suddenly she stopped and looked around the other way, out of the window on her side. There was a man standing there in the road. I didn't know him then, but it was Mr. Sutton.

"He looked just the way he did that time we saw him out at the oil well. He hadn't shaved, and he had the gun in his arm and was carrying a dead squirrel by the tail.

"He stood there looking at us for a minute with that awful, filthy grin, and then he said, 'Well, girls, a little lovers' spat, huh?'

"I couldn't do or say anything. I wondered if I was going to faint or be ill right there in the car. And then she tore into him, cursing just like a man. I don't think I've ever heard such things as she called him. And all the time he just stood there and grinned. Then he said, 'Well, girls, I won't interrupt you. You go ahead and kiss and make up.' And then he walked on away.

"I don't know yet how I got away. I must have just grabbed my things and run, out into the timber. The next thing I knew I was all alone, lying in some leaves with my slacks and things in my arms, sobbing for breath. After a while I got up and put them back on over my bathing suit and started walking. I found the road all right, and a Negro woman in an old Ford came along and gave me a ride to town. When I got home Sister still hadn't returned, so I tore up the note I'd left. I would never tell anybody about it."

"And that was all?" I asked. "I mean, until he came and looked you up?"

"No." She shook her head. "That was just the beginning. The terrible part was the next day, and Monday. She didn't come back to town that night. Somebody at the boarding-house notified the Sheriff's office that she was missing, and late Sunday afternoon Sutton came to town and reported the car had been parked there in the river bottom all night.

He apparently didn't say anything about having seen it before or knowing whose it was, or anything. They went out there, and when they found her slacks and shoes in the car they decided she must have gone swimming, and had drowned. They started looking for her in the river.

"I was scared, Harry. I was scared to death. Twice I tried to get up the nerve to go to the Sheriff and tell him about it, but I just couldn't do it. How could I explain why I'd run off and left her? And then early Monday morning they found her. Right in that pool below the bridge. Only they didn't think she had been drowned. They said she might have been killed by a blow on the head."

I whistled softly. It was a mess, an ugly one. "Did they find out who did it?"

"No," she said. "Of course, I was frantic by then. Now I couldn't tell them I'd been down there. But nobody knew about it—except Sutton. Around noon on Monday, after they'd brought her to town, he came into the office. Mr. Harshaw was out and I was there alone. He pretended he didn't know who I was at first, and just said he wanted to borrow five hundred dollars. I was so scared I didn't know what I was doing, but I did ask him the usual questions, about security and co-signers, and so on, and got out the forms. And all the time he was watching me, as if he couldn't remember where he'd seen me before. Somehow— I'll never know how—I got the papers ready for him to sign. And that was when he did it.

"Just as he picked up the pen, he pretended to recognize me. 'Now, I've got it,' he said. 'I knew I'd seen you some- where before, and I couldn't figure out how I'd forget a pretty girl like you.' You know that awful grin he has. 'It's too bad about your lady friend, isn't it? I wonder if they'll ever find out who did it?'

"Harry, I couldn't do anything. I couldn't think. I had to hold on to the counter to keep from falling, I was so weak. He said, 'But I'll tell you something that's a scream. They're looking for a *man*. Ain't that a laugh, baby?'

"Then he put down the pen, without signing the papers, and said, 'I'll tell you what, honey. All this paper work looks too complicated for an old country boy like me, what with all this fine print and stuff, so why don't you just give me the money now and you can fix up the fiduciaries and the hereinbefores yourself, like the smart little cookie you are. You see, I want to get out of town before that dam' Sheriff drives me crazy. Just because I live down there he keeps pestering me with a bunch of silly questions about whether I saw anybody else or another car, until honestly I'm just in a pet about it.' Then he winked at me and said, 'How about it, sweetie-pie? You'd do that for a nasty old man, wouldn't you?' "

She stopped and ran a hand across her face.

I'd told her I wasn't going to do anything except talk to him, but now I could feel a cold and terrible rage churning around inside me. I wanted to get my hands on him so bad they hurt.

"So he went out without signing it?" I asked. "And he got the money?"

"Yes. I told you I was a coward, Harry. I was in such a panic I couldn't think. So I had to falsify the books, to cover it up. Naturally, I didn't have that much money myself. But it was all right. I'd pay it back a little at a time, until I got it paid off."

"And then, the very next day, the Sheriff's office said they were convinced it was just an accident. They found a big snag in the pool under the bridge, just under the surface, and they believed she had dived off the bridge railing and hit it. It had either killed her outright or knocked her unconscious and she'd drowned. You see, they'd performed an autopsy Monday afternoon, and found a little water in her lungs. If she'd been dead when she fell into the water there probably wouldn't have been any."

She stopped.

"Well, look," I said, "then there isn't anything Sutton can do. The whole thing was an accident——"

She shook her head wearily. "You don't know Sutton, Harry. He came back a week later and got two hundred dollars more. Don't you see? He knew it wasn't my money I'd given him the first time, so now he had me there too.

And he was sure I was coward enough to keep on paying him to keep that ugly story from coming out. Don't you see the suspicion there'd always be if people knew? Maybe it was an accident. And maybe it wasn't."

She was right. It was sweet, and it was murder. Sutton had it figured from start to finish. And now he'd gouged her for over fifteen hundred dollars, adding a little at a time, so she could never get it all paid back. The only way she could cover it up was with phony loans which called for interest, so trying to whittle down the actual shortage, with this interest and Sutton's continued bites, was like trying to swim upstream over Niagara.

I gathered her up and kissed her. "All right, you can quit worrying about it. There won't be any more 'loans' to Sutton. And between the two of us we can put every nickel of it back and have the books straight in less than three months."

I wasn't as optimistic about it as I sounded, but I wanted to get the load off her mind right then, so she could get some rest.

"But, Harry, I've got to go to Mr. Harshaw——"

"No, honey," I said. "You can't. Don't you see, with his heart in the shape it's in, you can't tell him anything like that now? When it's all over and we're square with the world you can tell him if you want, but I don't see any sense in it. Actually, he'll have been making money on it at around three per cent per month for a year, so he should kick."

"But——" she protested, "there isn't any reason for you to get mixed up in it—paying it back, I mean."

"Yes," I said. "I can think of one. Maybe I mentioned it before. I'm in love with you."

For the first time, she smiled. It wasn't much, and she had to work at it awfully hard, but it was there and to me it looked like the sun coming up.

"Come on," I said. "Let's look for tear stains. I'm going to take you home, and I don't want your sister to think I've been beating you."

I switched on the light, and she repaired the damage.

While she was poking around in her purse, something fell
out of it, bounced once on the seat, and fell on to the floor
mat. I groped around for it and found it for her. It was a
money clasp, apparently of sterling silver and made in the
shape of a dollar sign.

"Say that's a pretty thing," I said.

"My mother gave it to me when I graduated from high
school."

I handed it back to her and she dropped it into her purse.
"We can be married any time," I said. "We've already got
our silver started."

She laughed, and finished rubbing out the tear stains. She
felt a lot better, and I kept on clowning so she wouldn't
know the way I was raging inside.

When I left her at the gate it was like pulling off an arm
to let her go, but I was anxious to get started before she
thought to ask me what I was going to do. I didn't want to
lie to her any more than I had to, and I knew she'd be
frantic and try to make me promise if she got an inkling of
what was going on in my mind.

When I got over on Main I stopped under a street light
and got out and opened the trunk. I found what I was
looking for, and threw them in the front seat. They were a
pair of leather gloves I'd won on a punchboard one time
and kept in the car for changing tyres. They were leather
all over, very thick and tough. For a job like this they'd
save your hands almost as well as having them taped.

I was doing seventy by the time I got out of town. I'd
forgotten about Tate and the Sheriff and the fact that they
were still keeping an eye on me. If they tried to follow me,
they got lost. I had to slow down when I left the highway,
but I was crowding it all the way across the sandhills and
through the river bottom. I went up over the second ridge
bucking along like a madman in the uneven ruts, and when
I hit the clearing I drove right up in his yard. And he
wasn't home.

The car was gone, and in the beams of the headlights I
could see the cabin door was closed. I sat there cursing for

two or three minutes before I remembered it was Saturday night. A big sport like Sutton would be in town, or even in the county seat. He had to spend all that easy money some way.

There was no use going back and looking for him around the beer joints and pool halls. The only thing to do was wait. I looked at my watch. It was a little after eleven.

I waited until twelve. And then it was one a.m. Somewhere far off a train whistled for a crossing, and once in a while a little night breeze would rustle through the oaks around the clearing. What was the use of hanging around any longer? He was probably bedded down somewhere by this time and wasn't coming back.

I gave it up finally at two-thirty and went back to town. I took a shower and lay down in the darkness with an all-night pass on the merry-go-round. The ash-tray on the floor beside the bed filled up and overflowed, and the sheets stuck to me every time I'd turn. I'd think of him, not satisfied with squeezing her dry with blackmail but having to dress it up with that crawling joke of his and humiliate her for his own particular brand of laughs, and the anger would come boiling up and choke me.

When was it going to end, and where? If I got him stopped, how about Dolores Harshaw? The whole thing was changed now. I wanted to stay here, and I wanted to marry Gloria. So then she'd just wish us luck, and that Sheriff would get off my back and take up raising orchids? There wasn't any way to guess what she was going to do.

I must have dropped off to sleep sometime towards dawn, for the next thing I knew it was ten-thirty and I could hear church-bells ringing. Sutton was back in my mind with the opening of my eyes, as if he'd never been gone, and even while I was looking at my watch I was rolling out of bed. I dressed and went downtown. Sunlight was brassy in the streets, stabbing at my eyes. Only a few people were in the restaurant. I ordered orange juice and coffee, and while I sat drinking it a man in a white hat came in and sat down at the second stool on my left. It was Tate. He nodded.

"How's it going?" I asked.

"All right, I guess."

"Anything new in the bank deal?"

"No," he said. "We're still waiting." He looked at me, the level gaze devoid of any expression at all, and then went back to the newspaper. "Just waiting."

I finished the coffee and put some change on the counter. "See you around," I said, and went out. I could feel him there behind me. Waiting, I thought. They'd wait a long time. I threw my cigarette savagely into the street and headed for the car, forgetting them. He ought to be home by now.

When I crossed the bridge over the river I thought of last night, and of her telling me, and began to ride the accelerator. And then when I hit the clearing I could see the car parked near the porch. He was home. I rolled to a stop in the front yard, grabbed the leather gloves off the seat, and got out.

I went up on the front porch and in the door without knocking. He wasn't there. I stood in the middle of the room, looking around, feeling the wicked proddings of impatience and baffled rage. It looked about the same as it had that other time, when I'd come out here with Gloria, the bed unmade and dirty dishes sitting on the table by the rear door. Maybe he'd gone hunting. I turned, looking along the walls. The .22 rifle was lying in a rack near the front door and just above it was a pump shotgun. He couldn't have gone far. A sudden thought occurred to me and I went over and checked the guns. The .22 was empty, but when I worked the action on the shotgun it was loaded. I jacked the three shells out on to the floor, picked them up, and threw them under the bed.

I sat down on the bed and leaned back against the wall. Outside I could hear a woodpecker hammering on a tree. The air was dead and very hot and I could feel sweat breaking out on my face. And then I heard him coming. He was climbing out of the ravine behind the house. I sat there as he appeared in the rear door, carrying a bucket of water in each hand.

He was wearing overalls, but no shirt, and the black hair

on his arms and chest glistened with sweat. The smooth
moon face split open with a grin that didn't get as far as his
eyes.

"Come in," he said. "Make yourself at home."

"Sure," I said. I pulled a foot back and put it behind the
edge of the small table beside the bed and shoved. It shot
across the room and crashed into the kitchen table. An ash-
tray rolled, spilling butts, and the kerosene lamp hit the
floor and shattered. Oil spilled down between the planks.
"Sit down," I said.

He looked at the mess. "Tough, huh?" He set the buckets
of water on a bench by the door.

"Yes," I said. "Tough."

His eye drifted towards the shotgun.

"It's not loaded," I said.

"Well, what'll they think of next?" He looked at me.
"What are we going to talk about? Not that I'm nosey, you
understand——"

"Gloria Harper. You've been on her back a little over a
year now——"

"And you came all the way out here to tell me to get off?
Is that it?"

"I'm going to do better than that," I said. "I'm going to
help you off."

I got up off the bed and started for him. He waited, not
even putting his hands up. I walked in on him, watching
the hands, and when they did move at last, the left feinting
at my face, I turned sharply on my left foot and took the
knee against my thigh. Maybe he was expecting somebody
from the Golden Gloves, I thought, swinging very low and
hard into his belly and moving in with it at the end. He
bent over, sucking for air and sick, and I put the glove in
his face and twisted it. He groped for me with a left, and I
hooked a right to his face which spilled him on to the edge
of the kitchen table. The legs caved in on one end and he
slid down it, getting mixed up with the plates and a bottle
of syrup. He tried to get up, the wind roaring in his throat,
and I dropped him again. It was five times before he stayed
down. I was winded and my hands hurt, and sweat ran

down my face like rain. I got him by the bib of the overalls and hauled him up against the slant of the table-top with my knee in his belly and bounced his head against it three times more for a sales talk and then let him slide down and roll around in the dishes. He was a mess to look at. I went over to the water buckets, fighting to get my breath, and poured water over the gloves to get the blood off, then took one of his shirts off the wall and dried them, and threw it on the floor. I poured the rest of the bucket of water in his face.

When I thought he could hear me, I squatted down beside him. "Now get this," I said. "You can't make trouble for her. But even if you could, there's nothing you can do to me. I'll still be here. And hell won't be big enough to hold you. So if you want to go around the rest of your life singing to yourself and slobbering down the front of your shirt, go ahead and try it."

I went out and got in the car and drove back to town. Maybe I'd sold him, and maybe I hadn't. The only thing I knew for sure was that next time I'd never get a chance to unload the shotgun.

16

THAT NEXT WEEK was wonderful. We didn't see anything of
Sutton, and we were together nearly all the time. We had
lunch together every day, and I spent a lot of time in the
loan office under the pretext of familiarizing myself with
the setup. When the other girl was gone we'd turn on to the
phony notes, trying to get them organized and establish
some sort of pattern for paying them off. She didn't want to
be married until the last one was paid.

"It isn't just stubbornness, Harry," she explained earnestly. "It has to be that way. You want me to quit work
when we're married, and we both know I can't quit till all
these are paid. They're my debt, and I have to pay them."

I had to admit she was right, in spite of my impatience.
We couldn't let somebody else take charge of the books
until they were in order. I thought of the twelve thousand
dollars buried in that old barn, just sitting there, and
wanted to go right out and dig it up and pay off the whole
fifteen hundred dollars at once. It didn't take much
thought, however, to throw that out. It wouldn't do. And it
might be very dangerous. In the first place, how could I
explain to her where I'd suddenly got hold of that much
money? And worse than that, I couldn't be absolutely sure
the Sheriff had been lying when he'd said the bank had the
serial numbers of it. It would be suicide to try to run the
stuff right back through the same bank it'd come out of,
and this soon afterwards. I'd just be asking for it. That
money was going to stay there a long time, maybe for
years, and when it went back into circulation it would be a
long way from here. I'd have to think of something. But I
didn't worry about it; I had plenty of time....

At odd moments I did some digging back into sales records on the lot, and I could see that even if I couldn't build it up I'd still clear five or six hundred dollars a month with the commissions and the salary he was paying me. And I was working on a number of ideas for whooping sales up if we could get the cars. There wasn't too much live competition around here, even in the county seat, and with some advertising and good promotion to stir it up there was no reason we couldn't nearly double the business.

The hardest part, of course, was going to be the waiting. We added it all up, and by pooling every nickel we'd make and could spare it would still take until sometime in November to get it all paid off. We wouldn't have anything left to start with, but I'd have a good job and somehow we'd scrape up enough for at least a week's honeymoon in Galveston.

Once or twice she got scared and despondent again, thinking of Sutton, but I was able to talk her out of it. She asked me what I'd done and I was as evasive about it as I could be without making her suspicious. I told her I'd had a talk with him and warned him, which was true as far as it went.

It wasn't always so easy at night though, after I'd left her and was lying there in my room. We hadn't seen anything of him, but how did I know we wouldn't? Everything we had planned was based on the assumption that I'd scared him off and there wouldn't be any more demands. So what if I was wrong? And there was always Dolores Harshaw. I didn't know what she was going to do about it.

I think it was Tuesday night when it hit me. I was lying there in the dark going around with it for the thousandth time, trying to guess whether she'd meant it or not and what my chances would be if she pulled her alibi out from under me and dropped me back into that hellhole of questions, when suddenly I sat up in bed with the whole answer perfectly clear in my mind. She didn't have me. I had her. She couldn't do a thing.

I thought about it for a while, and then turned over and dropped off into an untroubled sleep for the first time in weeks. If she tried anything she was going to get the surprise of her life.

I went out to see Harshaw Friday night to give him a short rundown on how we'd been doing. He looked a little better. He was still weak and shaky, but the dirty grey colour had cleared up and he appeared to be becoming reconciled to inactivity. He was sitting in the living-room reading "Lee's Lieutenants" while she listened to some quiz show on the radio.

I made the business talk as brief as possible, not playing up the advertising ideas too much because I didn't want to run the risk of starting an argument and getting him heated up. He grunted more or less approvingly at most of the details, and nodded once or twice. "Sounds all right," he said. "I guess you'll make out."

"I think so," I said. She had turned off the radio and was wandering restlessly around the room. I could see she was bored, and I wondered what she'd try next. But I wasn't afraid of her any more.

"How are you getting along with Miss Harper?" he asked.

I grinned. "I remembered what you told me. We're going to be married in November, so I'll be able to mistreat her all I want."

He gave me that probing look, and then his face softened a little. I thought he was going to smile. "Marry her, huh? You're beginning to show signs of intelligence. When you get that girl it'll be the best day's work you ever did."

"I know it," I said. I happened to look up at her just then. She was behind him, adjusting the venetian blinds. She turned and looked at me with that malicious smile on her face.

"I think that's wonderful," she said. "She's such a sweet girl."

"Thank you," I said.

"I know you'll both be very happy." The smile slipped a little and you could see past it. She was raging. I wondered how long it'd be before I heard from her.

It wasn't very long. It was that same night.

It was around midnight. I was coming back from taking Gloria home and as I pulled up in front of the rooming house another car came up behind me. I stepped out, and it came up alongside and stopped. A voice said softly, "Get in," and I knew who it was. I got in. It would be the last time.

She went on around the block and over to Main, turning north and gunning it fast along the highway. "How's the happy bridegroom?" she asked.

"Not bad," I said.

"But I'm rushing it a little, aren't I? You're not a bridegroom yet; you're just engaged. You're lovely, and you're engaged. Isn't that sweet?"

"Yes," I said. "And what's on your mind?"

"You'd never guess, would you?"

"I thought I told you the last time. We're through."

"We are like hell. Remember?"

She pulled off on to a side road and stopped.

"Well," she said, "so I'm just going to sit around on my hands and let you and that angel-faced candy kid get away with it, am I? The two of you're just too cute for anything. You make me sick."

"Go ahead," I said. "Tell me all about it. And when you get through I'll tell you."

"You're not going to marry her. In November, or any other time. I thought we'd straightened that out already."

"You've got some other plan in mind?"

"You're damned right I have. You're going to marry me."

"I thought the bag limit was one husband at a time."

"Maybe I'm thinking of getting a divorce."

It was something about the way she said it. She didn't mean divorce. Or I didn't think she did. It was just an awful feeling that I was very close to knowing, for the first time, what she was really driving at. She could have left him any time, and he'd probably give her a divorce whenever she asked for it. Maybe she was waiting for more. He'd had two heart attacks—It was a little sickening.

"All right," I said. "Get a divorce. But not on my account. I've told you what I'm going to do."

"You think I'm bluffing, don't you?"

"I wouldn't know."

"What do you suppose the Sheriff'll do when he finds out what really happened that day?"

"So you're going to tell him?"

"Certainly I am."

"And have you thought over what's going to happen when you do?"

"What do you mean?"

"You'll go to jail."

"Who do you think you're kidding?"

"Nobody. If I committed a crime, you're an accessory to it. I say *if* I committed one. You don't know, you see. But if I did, now you're as guilty as I am. You not only withheld evidence, but you lied about it."

"I don't believe you." She was still loud and defiant and angry, but I could hear a little note of uncertainty creeping in.

"Well, I've told you," I said. "But if you're such a hot-shot hard guy, go ahead and try it. Personally, I don't think they could convict either one of us of anything, but it'd certainly give people something to talk about. Such as, why did you lie about seeing me there in the first place? And what's been going on, girls, that we didn't know anything about?"

"Why you dirty——"

"Well, I just thought I'd tell you, pal, before your neck got out another foot. You'd better reel it in."

"So that's the way it is?"

"That's exactly the way it is."

"All right," she said. "I'll tell you what I think of it. And you. And everything about you. And her."

She told me.

She was still telling me when she slid the wheels to slow down a little to let me out three blocks away from the rooming house. I didn't mind walking. It gave my ears a chance to stop ringing, and gave me a breather to let the fact soak in that I was through with her at last. It was wonderful. Everything was wonderful.

It was a happy few hours. The next morning at ten o'clock Sutton walked into the office to see me.

Gulick was up the street having coffee. I was at my desk doing some paper-work when I heard the car stop outside on the lot. I'd just shoved the papers aside and started to get up to see who it was when he walked in the door. He pulled a chair over and sat down in front of the desk. His face was still a mess, but I didn't pay much attention to it. I was watching his hands. He didn't have on a coat and I couldn't see any place he could be carrying a gun, but if he did have one I didn't have a chance, with that desk between us. By the time I got to him it wouldn't make any difference whether I got there or not.

He fished in the breast pocket of his shirt for a cigarette and then reached down. I waited, scarcely breathing. When the hand came out of his pants pocket it held nothing but a big kitchen match. He raked it along the edge of the desk and lighted his cigarette.

"Don't mind the way my face looks," he said. "I fell out of bed. I was having a funny dream."

"What's on your mind?" I asked.

"That's the way to do business," he said, with what might have been a grin. His face was so puffed and cut not much of it moved. "Always get right to the point. Well, I'll tell you. I'm thinking of buying another car pretty soon."

"How about just paying for the one you've got now?" I said.

"Oh. That's all right. I'll trade it in on the new one."

"Like perpetual motion, huh? You want to trade in a car you don't own for another one you can't pay for. You ought to be in the government."

"It must rub off on you," he said. "You've been a big shot less than a week and you sound just like Harshaw already."

"Maybe I was wrong," I said. "You ought to work for the newspaper."

"Oh, I take an interest in things. But how about the car? I've kind of got my eye on that Buick up there at the end."

"That's twenty-four hundred dollars worth of car. Eight hundred down. What are you using for money?"

"I told you. I'll trade mine."

I was beginning to get fed up with it. It didn't look as if he had a gun or was looking for trouble, and I couldn't figure out what he was getting at.

"Cut it out," I said. "If you haven't got anything to do, I have. Your equity in that Ford is about three hundred dollars, and we both know how you got that much in it. And just to jog your memory, that gravy-train has quit running." I stopped and looked at him. "Incidentally, your next note is two or three days overdue, so unless you've got fifty-five dollars on you you'd better start thinking about walking home. Thanks for bringing it in."

"Oh, that's all right," he said. "But you still don't catch on. Why should I make another payment on it when I'm going to turn it back? On that Buick. Let's go take a ride in it. We can work out the down payment then."

I started to tell him to beat it when I looked up and saw Gulick coming back. There was no use letting him get an earful. "O.K.," I said. I got the key out of the drawer. "Let's take a ride."

We went out to the car. "Mind if I drive?" he asked.

"No. Go ahead."

I climbed in beside him and he eased it out into Main. "Nice car," he said. "Radio and everything, huh?"

"Now listen, you stupid bastard," I said, "I don't know what you're driving at, but I can get a bellyful of you quicker than most people. So why don't you get wise and shove? You fall out of that bed about once more and the grasshoppers'll start talking to you."

"You know," he said, "I been thinkin about that." He turned right beyond the bank and started down the street where the Taylor building had been. "Thought I might go out to the Coast."

"Now you're getting smart."

He jerked his head towards the charred rubble and the ashes. "Quite a fire they had, wasn't it?"

"Yeah," I said. I'll never know why I didn't begin to tumble then. Maybe it was that silly, half-witted act he was putting on.

He turned again at the second cross street and started around the block. And just after he'd made the last turn he pulled to the kerb and stopped. We were facing up the street towards what had been the rear of the Taylor building. There was a big elm hanging out over the kerb and we were in the shade. There was something awfully familiar about it. And then the warning began to go off in my head at last. This was the exact spot where I'd parked the car that day of the fire. The chill was going all over me now in spite of the midmorning heat. There wasn't one chance in a thousand he'd stumbled on this spot accidentally. And the only way he could have known about it—I didn't want to think about that.

"You know, it's funny about this place," he said. "Familiar, sort of; ain't it? You ever get that feeling? You know, that you've been in a place before."

"Break it up," I said. "What are you talking about?"

"That day they had the fire. Seems to me I was walking along here, going back to town, about a half hour after it started. I'd been over there watching it, see, but I'm kind of funny; fires bore me after a while. The way I see it, there's no money in 'em. Or at least that's what I thought then. That just shows you how stupid a man can be when he don't use his head. Now, you take a smart son-of-a-bitch like you, a real big-shot sort of guy, he knows there's money in fires."

"How about getting to it?" I said. "It wouldn't take much to finish that face for you."

He lighted a cigarette and shook his head. The simpleton act was gone now. "I wouldn't advise it, pal. You know how the monkey was caught in the lawn-mower. The best thing to do in a case like that is to hold still."

"Hold still for what?" I asked, feeling the sweat gathering on my face.

"Well, let's say about five thousand, plus the Buick. They say you tapped the bank for ten, which probably means about fifteen grand, so I figure around half will do for me. The way I see it, why be a hog? People wouldn't like you."

"I think I'm beginning to get it," I said. "You've got a goofy idea I had something to do with that bank business, and so——"

"Let's just skip all that part, pal," he said. I could see I was boring him. "Let's just talk about the geetus. It's more fun that way. As far as thinking you clouted the bank, you're talking about the Sheriff and that deputy, Tate. They think you did it. Me, I'm another guy altogether. I just happen to be the only one who can prove it. But we wouldn't want to make it that easy for 'em, would we, pal? As I see it, let 'em earn their money. So that being the case——"

"You keep talking, but you haven't said anything," I broke in. "What do you mean, you can prove a crazy pipe dream like that?"

"Just like I said. I saw you drive up here in a hell of a hurry thirty minutes after the fire broke out and everybody who wasn't staying for the second show had started home——"

"What does that prove?" I said angrily. "Maybe I was supposed to punch a time-clock, or something?"

"Please, pal. Keep your stories straight. I can see you're just breaking in. You tell them you got there with the fire-wagon, and now you tell me you can come dragging in any time you want. You got to tell everybody the same story, see. I get in more trouble with girls that way. Of course, I run around with more the female type of girl myself."

I went for him, but he saw it in my face before I got started. His hand slipped inside the shirt, under his right armpit, and came out with it. It was a woman's gun, a little pearl-handled automatic, not as big as his hand as he let it rest in his lap, but there's no difference between being killed with one of them and with a .45 unless it's prestige you're after.

I slid back and left him alone.

17

"Now," HE SAID, "let's talk about the geetus."

He'd deliberately needled me into lunging for him so he could flash that gun. It made him feel better—that and the way he had sucked me out of position with that simpleton act of his.

"Let's get this straight," I said. "You really expect me to give you five thousand dollars I haven't got and a Buick that doesn't belong to me?"

He shook his head. "Let's cut out the horsing around. You go dig up that dough from wherever you hid it and slice me five grand off the little end, nothing bigger than twenties. Then you make out the papers on this car, take mine in on the down payment, and you can take care of the notes any way you want.

"You see, pal," he went on, "you're in a worse spot than it looks like at first. Remember what you told me? If I didn't quit touching Goldilocks for a sawbuck now and then for beer money you'd slap me around till I started shuffling my feet and talking back to the bedbugs. Because you'd be around here to do it. But the catch is, you won't. You'll be up the river trying to think up a spiel to give the parole board in 1971, and wondering how Sweetie-pie is making out in the sawbuck department.

"You catch on? I can't lose either way. But you sure as hell can if you don't go along with me. So just shell out, like I told you, and I'll take off for the Coast. You'll still have half of it left, so you can settle down and join the Chamber of Commerce and talk about the dirty crooks in Washington."

And I'd thought he was stupid. I sat there feeling the sick

emptiness inside me and listening to him drive the nails in it one at a time. He had me any way I could turn, and he wasn't bluffing. As he said, he won either way. There wasn't any way out. They still might not prove it when they picked me up again, but all the odds were on their side. They'd know now for sure and without any doubt at all, and there wouldn't be anybody to spring me this time before the questions drove me crazy. Harshaw would fire me, and Dolores Harshaw might have to get on the stand and admit she'd lied. All that business would come out, and it'd settle me with Gloria. He was right. There not only wasn't any way he could lose; there wasn't any way I could win.

"Look," I said at last, "how do I know you'll go?"

"You don't, pal." He tried to grin with that messed-up face. "You'll just have to take my word for it."

"Well, geez," I said. "I've got to have a little time. I've got to think it over. You're pulling all this stuff on me, and I can't figure out whether I'm up or down——"

"There's nothing to think over. Just take my word for it, pal. You're down."

"Yeah, but—Look. I'm not admitting a thing, understand, but even if I had that kind of money it'd take me a while to get hold of it. And the car—It's almost noon Saturday, and we can't get the paper-work done on it today."

"That's all right. I notice there's a dent in the right rear fender, anyway, and I want that fixed. I'm not in that big a hurry; I can pick it up from you on Monday. You're not going anywhere; you know what'll happen if you try to run."

He stopped talking and turned to look at me out of eyes sunk back in that scrambled and puffed-up face. "A real neat package," he said. "Isn't it, pal?"

The long, hot Saturday afternoon was an endless hell of sitting at the desk looking at papers I didn't even see while everything tumbled around me. The finishing touch had come at noon, when I picked Gloria up to take her to lunch. One glance at her face was all it took. He'd been to see her too. We sat in a booth in the crowded restaurant, unable to talk about it for fear of being overheard, while we looked at the ruin of everything we had planned. She couldn't know what he'd told me, and I didn't say anything about it, but she didn't have to to understand the spot we were in. All that mattered was that he was back again for more and all our bright ideas for getting the books straightened out by November or any other time were shot to hell. I tried to cheer her up, but it was useless.

I'd see her that night, but what was the use? What could I say? That he'd promised to leave, and go to California? That was too stupid to repeat. There was a fat chance he'd go off and leave a gravy-train like this. This was just the opening wedge. He'd stick around until he got it all, and then he'd stay right on, milking both of us for what we made or what we had to steal to keep his big mouth shut.

Why had he waited all this time? I couldn't even figure that out. I shuffled unseen papers in the heat, thinking, going around and around in the same smooth rut from which there was no escape. I hadn't even got to the worst part of it yet. Suppose he got the money. Suppose he got all of it. That still wasn't it. *It* was what was going to happen the minute he got his hands on it. He'd start throwing it around, making a big show around the beer joints and pool halls, and that was exactly what that cold-eyed Sheriff was waiting for, some citizen with too much sudden prosperity. They'd pick him up, and to get out from under he'd tell 'em where he got it. So in paying him off to keep out of jail, I'd just be buying a one-way ticket right into the place.

I picked her up a little after seven and we drove out into the country and parked the car on a side road. I held her in my arms for a long time, not talking, and at last she stirred a little and looked up at me so hopelessly it was like a knife turning inside me.

"He wanted five hundred dollars," she said.

"Did you give it to him?"

"Not yet," she said dully. "I told him we didn't have it in the safe, and the bank was closed."

"Good," I said. "We'll think of something."

"We have to, Harry," she said. "He said he'd go away. He said he was going out west. If we give it to him, maybe he'll stay away."

I wasn't thinking, or I'd have kept my big mouth shut. "Like hell he will. Blackmailers are all the same. Every bite is always the last—until the next one."

"I know. But what can we do? He *might* go."

"He won't. And we won't get anywhere by paying him. The thing to do is stop him."

"But how?" she asked frantically. Then she thought of something. "Harry, did you do that to his face? I never saw anything so—so horrible."

"Yes," I said. "I won't lie to you. I did it. And a fat lot of good it did."

"I hate that sort of thing, Harry. You won't do it again, will you?"

"All right. It didn't do any good, anyway."

"We'll just have to give him what he wants, and hope he'll leave."

"He'll never leave if you give him what he wants," I said.

"Then you don't want me to give him the money?" she asked.

"No," I said. "Don't give him anything till I tell you to."

"What are you going to do, Harry?"

"I don't know yet, baby. I just don't know."

"Darling, please tell me why you don't want to give it to him. Isn't that the best thing to do?"

"It's the very worst thing we could do. The way to get a blackmailer off your back is to stop him, not pay him."

"What do you mean? How can we stop him?"

"I don't know yet," I said. "But you just leave it to me."

I took her home around midnight and went back to the rooming house. I lay in bed thinking about it, and after a while I was conscious that I was no longer wondering what to do. I was thinking of how to do it. Sometime during the afternoon or evening I had already arrived at the only answer there could ever be to Sutton. I was going to kill him.

How?

The match flared as I lighted another cigarette. I could see the face of the wrist watch. It was nearly two-thirty.

There was no use trying to kid myself. It was dangerous, It was dangerous as hell. I thought of that Sheriff. Anybody who committed a crime in his county was taking a long, long chance. And I already had one strike on me. He had his eye on me. I was a marked man, and he was probably having me watched. I had to get down there and do it and get back without Tate's knowing I had left town.

How?

I rolled over on my back and lay staring up at the ceiling. I not only had to get past the Sheriff; I had to fool Gloria. There was no telling what a thing like that would do to her. She'd probably crack up if she ever found it out.

How? How? How?

And what about Sutton himself? I knew by this time I was dealing with no fool. He was plenty smart, and he was armed. I thought about the guns. He had that Junior League automatic, a .22 rifle, and a shotgun. And then I began to get it.

I sat up in bed.

It didn't come to me all at once. It took a long time to work it all out, step by step, thinking of all the possibilities and when I was through it was dawn. It was a hot, breathless dawn, the way it is before a storm, and as the sun came up I looked out across the back yard at the high board fence splashed with crimson. Red in the morning, I thought, sailor take warning.

It meant nothing except that it would probably rain by tonight. I turned on my side and went to sleep.

I awoke around noon with a bad taste in my mouth and my body drenched with perspiration. Outside the sun was a brassy glare, and there was no whisper of a breeze. I walked uptown and bought the Houston paper and took it into the restaurant, propping it up before me while I drank some orange juice. I remembered none of the news, even while I was reading it, but this had to look like any other Sunday. I was tight and nervous, for I could feel that cold-eyed Sheriff looking over my shoulder at every move I made. It had to be natural from start to finish, for he had a merciless eye for anything that didn't fit.

It was a day that would never end. Around five o'clock I drove over to the Robinsons', but Gloria had gone out about an hour ago, they said. I talked to them for a few minutes, and then left, unable to sit still. Time crawled. Tension was building up already, and I still had hours to go.

I went back about seven and she was home. She'd gone for a ride to try to cool off, she said. We went over to the county seat to an air-conditioned movie, trying to escape our thoughts and the heat. On the way home she was depressed and silent and nothing I could do would bring her out of it. There was a feeling she was more than usually upset by Sutton and that she wanted to tell me something, but she never did. When we got back to town she said she had a headache and wanted to go to bed early. I left her at the gate.

I parked the car in front of the rooming house and went on through to my room. I was going to stay there all night, just in case Tate had orders to check on me from time to time. Looking at my watch, I saw it was almost eleven. I changed clothes, putting on dark slacks, a blue sports shirt, and black shoes. I left the light burning for a while, as if I were reading, and after about a half hour I turned it out and lay down on the bed. The landlady's room was directly above mine, and I could see the light from her window shining out into the back yard. In another twenty minutes it went out.

I waited. The whole house was deathly still now. I tried to quiet my nerves by thinking how it would be afterwards, of Galveston and a honeymoon in November, and all the years ahead. It would work for a few minutes and then I'd be tightened up again, thinking of what had to be done first, of Sutton lying there in the cabin, waiting for me maybe, or at least alert and knowing the risk he was running, and of the gun which wouldn't be very far from his hand. And then I'd think of the Sheriff and the fact that this time the game we were playing wasn't only for keeps, but forever. It made me cold thinking about it, but there wasn't any other way. Sutton had asked for it. He'd get it.

I struck a match and looked at my watch. It was an hour since the landlady's light had gone out. I got softly off the bed and stood up. It was time to go.

THERE WAS A SCREEN DOOR leading from my room into the backyard. I eased it open, an inch at a time, and slipped out, and closed it very gently. The night was heavily overcast and so dark I couldn't see the gate. I knew where it was, though, and moved towards it, keeping on the grass to muffle any sound. Then my hands were on the gate, feeling for the latch. I opened it and eased out into the alley.

I went over to the car lot, walking fast and avoiding street lights, and slipped up to it from the rear. I eased around the corner of the shack, put the key in the lock, and stepped inside, closing the door after me. I didn't need any light to find the cigar box which held the ignition keys; it was in the top drawer of my desk and I located it by feel. Carrying it over to a corner away from the windows, I squatted down so my body would shield the flame, and struck a match. All the keys had round cardboard tags with numbers on them, and it took me only a second or two to find the one I wanted. It was the key to the Ford which was parked down at the end of the line where the shadows were heaviest and I could pull right out into the cross street without going on to Main at all. I put the others back in the desk and slipped out and closed the door.

I stood between two cars and peered out, looking up Main. A block and a half up the lights of the restaurant poured out into the night, but there was no one on the street. The constable would be inside, probably, drinking coffee. I ducked back and climbed into the Ford, reaching for the starter. The motor turned over slowly, as if the battery was weak. I jabbed it again, and it caught this time.

It's all right, I thought. Driving out there will charge it
up. I got it in gear and rolled out into the cross street, not
turning on the lights until I was off the lot. Going over two
blocks, I turned left and ran parallel to Main until I was in
the edge of town, and then cut back and got on the highway. There was very little traffic. I met only two or three
cars. I made the turnoff, feeling my stomach tighten up,
and started uphill through the pines. As I passed the old
farm I turned my head and looked towards the barn and
wished I'd never heard of the money that was buried there.

After I crossed the bridge over the river and climbed up
out of the bottom I slowed down, trying to remember all
the details of the road. I had to be careful not to get too
near. He'd hear the car. I stared intently ahead into the
beam of light, watching the wall of timber going past on
each side and disappearing into the blackness behind me.
Then just after I was over the crest of the ridge and starting
down I found what I wanted, a place where I could get the
car off the road on firm ground and pine needles which
wouldn't show the tracks. I pulled off and cut the motor,
leaving the key in the switch, and then turned off the lights.

Velvety, impenetrable blackness closed in around me. I
got out and closed the door and held my hand up in front
of my eyes. I couldn't see it. It was like being blind. I
groped my way back out to the road, and when I was out
from under the trees it was a little better.

A sudden thought occurred to me. How would I ever find
the car when I came back? In this ocean of blackness there
was nothing to mark the place I'd driven off the road. I took
out my handkerchief and dropped it beside the ruts. Out of
the corners of my eyes I could see it very faintly, a tiny blur
of grey.

It should be less than a quarter mile to the clearing. I
turned and faced downhill, feeling the tightness in my
chest and the rapid beating of my heart. For the first time I
noticed the charged and sullen vacuum of the night itself.
There were no stars, and the air had the hot, dead feel of a
closed and sealed-off room. Not a leaf moved. There were
no night sounds at all. Everything seemed to be waiting,

holding its breath for an explosion that might come any minute. Then in a moment there was a growl of thunder somewhere off in the west. It wouldn't be long.

I started downhill in the darkness, feeling my way and stumbling now and then in the ruts. Once I missed a turn and blundered off into the trees. Panic caught up with me for a minute. Suppose I lost the road? I'd never find my way out until daylight. And then the really horrible thought came sweeping over me. What if I lost it *afterwards*? If anyone saw me down here, or coming out of here, it could mean the electric chair. I cursed and tried to shake off the chill as I turned and stumbled back into the road.

How long had it been now? The road seemed to go on forever, winding down off the hill. Was I sure I was on the right one? I had to be. There wasn't any other. But I should have come to the clearing before this. The thunder was growing nearer. I wanted to run, and cursed myself, knowing how stupid it was. It's just the waiting, I thought. Once I get there I'll be all right. And then I was out in the clearing.

The shack would be around to the right, less than fifty yards away. I felt my way cautiously along the faint traces of the road. A long roll of thunder growled and reverberated across the sky, sounding very near. In a moment there was a jagged flash of lightning and I saw the cabin in the greenish-yellow, unnatural light, and then in the quick fraction of a second before it was gone I caught a glimpse of the car standing near the porch. Breath swelled up in my chest, making it painfully tight. He was home. Then blackness rolled back over everything like a breaking sea, and thunder crashed over the clearing.

Temporarily blinded by the lightning flash, I couldn't see anything now. It was like the bottom of a coal-mine. I groped my way ahead, moving in the direction I had seen the shack. Then it began to take shape, a dense pile of shadow a little nearer than the inky wall of trees behind it. I was very near the front porch. I could hardly breathe. The tension was almost unbearable. I located the door and stepped carefully up on to the porch, the rubber-soled shoes making no sound at all.

The bed, I thought—it's just inside the door, on the right. All I have to do is step inside and turn and reach down, and before he gets his hand on that gun I'll have mine on his throat and turn the blackmailing bastard off like a leaky faucet. I moved the other foot, easing it down like a cat. I was in the doorway, and then inside, and turning.

Everything fell apart at once and the night erupted into wildness. There was a sudden, brilliant flash of lightning which lit up the inside of the shack like a flash-bulb going off, and then it was gone and the thunder crashed at the same time. It shook the house, and through the roar and rattle of it I heard the sharp report of the gun as he fired. I was turning, and diving towards the floor, and as the blackness rolled back over us I saw the orange spurt of flame as he shot again, and then I was conscious that woven into all this madness of sound there was one more and that it was a woman screaming without beginning or end or drawing breath or changing pitch, going on and on through the dying roll of thunder and the crashing echo of the gun and the meaty impact as we slammed into each other and fell to the floor together and then the sound of the gun again. He was under me and I was trying to locate the flailing hand which had the gun and get hold of it before he could put it against me somewhere and shoot, and then the scream did change at last as she put her feet out of the bed and on top of us and fell beyond us on the floor. He shifted under me and whirled me over until we were both lying on our sides, and I felt something under my ribs and knew he didn't have the gun any more. He had let it slip out of his hand when I'd crashed into him, and now we were fighting on top of a loaded automatic with the safety off.

The scream was gone now, and I could hear the desperate sucking sound as she fought to get her breath, and the scrambling as she got up off the floor and ran out the back door into the timber just as the first drumming roar of the rain began, and then the two of us were alone, fighting silently on the floor near the edge of the bed. I located his face with my left hand and swung the right and felt the shock go up my arm as I landed on his jaw. He was clawing wildly for me and I hit him again, and this time he jerked a little and lay still. I shifted my hands down to his throat and began to tighten them to shut off the blackmail forever, right at its source, and then there was a voice somewhere inside me screaming over and over that something was wrong and I had to stop before it was too late. I didn't get it for a moment, and then when I did the strength went out of me and I turned him loose, cursing with a futile sort of rage. I couldn't do it now. Of course I couldn't. How could I, with a witness to it before it even happened?

I got to my knees, and felt around on the floor until I found the gun. Moving my hand across it until I located the safety, I clicked it off, and put it in my pocket, and then got up with the breath roaring in my throat, still raging, knowing I couldn't do it now and that I'd never get another chance, and that we were ruined, all on account of that crazy bitch of a woman, whoever she was, running around out there through the timber in the rain. She had seen me in the lightning flash, the same as he had, and if I killed him she could send me to the chair for it.

Because it made no difference at all now, I struck a match and looked around for the lamp. Then I remembered I'd broken it the last time I was out here, and was about to give up the idea when I suddenly saw it over on the kitchen table. He had bought a new one. I went over and lifted off the chimney and lighted it.

He hadn't moved. He was lying on his back with nothing on but a pair of zebra-striped shorts, and he could have been merely asleep because he was snoring. He'd whipped me. He'd ruined me. And he was lying on the floor sleeping like a baby. All because his girl friend was running around out there somewhere in the rain and I couldn't touch him.

Who was she? But what difference did it make? I jerked my head around and saw the wisp of pink tangled up with the kicked-back sheets on the bed and the shoes on the floor near the foot of it, and the purse lying open on the table. Well, I thought, she still has a dress to go home in, but it's going to get a little wet—— And then I stopped. *The shoes*. I swung back, staring.

They weren't shoes; they were wedgies. They were wedgies with grass straps. I stood there raking my hand across my face. So I had thought I was free of her! The dirty, lousy, rotten, sneaking, useless, trouble-making little tramp! So now I could wear Sutton round my neck for the rest of my life knowing she was the one who'd saved him.

I was suddenly tired, and wanted to sit down. I pulled a chair up alongside the table and collapsed into it, groping wearily for a cigarette. We were finished. There was no hope now. And all because of that I cursed futilely, hopelessly, listening to the wild drumming of the rain. I lighted the cigarette after a while and leaned over from force of habit to put the match in an ash-tray. I didn't see it there on the table, and idly caught hold of the purse to look behind it. It was open, and as it swung around I was looking into it. There was the usual hodge-podge of junk all mixed up in it, lipstick, comb, bobby pins and so on, but it was something shiny lying just behind it which caught my eye. Only a corner of it was sticking out in view. Hardly even knowing why I did it, I reached out and picked it up. I stared at it, blankly at first, and then unbelievingly, and at last with a cold and terrible deadliness that made the hair stand up along my neck. It was a money clasp, a silver money clasp in the shape of a dollar sign.

No! It was crazy. There must be more than one of them in the world. It was a coincidence. But even as I was telling myself it was, I knew it wasn't. I was beginning to see it. I was remembering the day Spunky was lost and I'd carried her shoes back to leave them on the sand-bank for him, thinking at the time they were the same as Dolores Harshaw's. Through the red mist in front of my eyes I could see it all now: the strange, unhappy way she'd acted tonight, the headache, wanting to go to bed early—— I cursed and jumped to my feet. His blue serge trousers were hanging on the wall. I grabbed them down, and rammed my hands into the pockets. There was nothing. I tried the overalls hanging beside them, without success. I looked wildly around. Maybe ... I lunged for the bed, stepping over him, and snatched up the pillow. The wallet was under it. I spread it open, and there it was, a thick sheaf of bills. My hands were shaking as I counted them. It came to a little over five hundred dollars.

So that was it. She had brought him the money he had asked for, but with that cynical brutality of his he wasn't shaking her down for money alone—— But why had she done it? I knew her better than that. She would have let him kill her first. And then, slowly and quite terribly, it began to dawn on me. He had told her about me, and about the bank, when he went to see her yesterday morning. She had begged me to let her give him the money, and I wouldn't. And even then, before I knew it myself, she was afraid I was going to kill him. She'd come out here and brought it, begging him to take it and go away. She hadn't been trying to save herself. It was me she was thinking of.

I was as cold as ice all over, and I could hardly get my breath. I thought of her out there trying to find her way back to her car through the rain and darkness, half petrified with terror and running into trees, and barefoot. I got up slowly and took the little automatic out of my pocket and stood there looking at him. When his head turned a little and he tried to move I squatted down beside him.

"Wake up," I said, my voice thick and unrecognizable. "Wake up and see what I've got for you."

He stirred and tried to raise up. When he saw me his eyes went wide and he tried to slide backwards, away from me. I got him by the throat with my left hand and put my knee in his belly and grinned at him. His mouth opened, wider and wider as he tried to scream, but no sound came out of it. His eyes were terrible to look at, and I laughed at him.

"Don't go away," I said, and raised the gun a little and shot him just over the left eye.

When the sound of the shot had died away there was nothing but the rain. I stood there looking down at all that was left of Sutton, still holding the gun in my hand, and some of the crazy wildness began to drain away. She would know it now, I thought. That seemed to be the only thing my mind would take hold of in that first minute or two. I hadn't wanted her to, but now she would.

I shook my head impatiently, trying to think. Why was I wasting time with some stupid thing like that? Sure, she'd know, *but she was the only one.* There wasn't any witness. This wasn't the way I'd planned to do it, but it was still all right. It was all right if I got hold of myself and did something besides standing here the rest of the night muttering to myself.

I had to get started, and I had to work fast. There was a lot to be done, and time was running out on me. I looked swiftly around the room as my head began to clear, thinking of my original plan. I'd intended to use the shotgun on him to cover it up, setting it up to look like an accident while he was cleaning the gun. The shotgun was out now, but the idea was still good.

I grabbed his overalls off the wall and hauled at him until I got them on him. Then I put on his shoes and laced them up. I looked at him. A little blood had come out of the place where the bullet had gone in, but none of it had run on to the floor. It was on his face. I pulled a chair up by the table, hoisted him up, and shoved him into it, and then let him slump forward with his face on the table.

I was all right now. My head was clear and I was working very efficiently. He didn't bother me. I didn't have any feeling about him at all. I had other things to think about— such as fingerprints.

I grabbed one of his shirts off the wall and had just started to clean off the lamp where I'd carried it, when I heard the car. It was somewhere across the clearing. I heard it start up, the motor racing, and then it started up the hill. She had made it. She was all right. That worry was off my mind now. I finished cleaning the lamp, then rubbed the shirt along the table and chair and the other things I'd touched. I went over to the gun racks and lifted down the shotgun, using the shirt so I wouldn't leave any prints on it. I worked the slide action until the magazine was emptied, picked the shells off the floor and placed them on the table, still being careful about touching anything with my bare fingers. Leaving the action open, I held it around to the light and looked down the barrel. It was clean. That was fine. I placed the gun across the table on his right, as if he'd just finished cleaning it and had started work on the little automatic when the accident happened. A man who has several guns never cleans and oils just one when he has the cleaning gear out. It would be like eating one peanut.

I straightened up, looking around. Where would he keep it? There was a locker nailed on the front wall near the gun racks. That looked like a good place. I opened it, using the shirt on the glass knob, and found what I was looking for, a can of gun oil, the rod he used for cleaning the shotgun, some oily rags and cut patches, and a can of solvent. I carried it all over and put it on the table.

I rubbed the automatic very carefully with the shirt to get my prints off. Then I wiped both his hands with one of the oily rags—because he'd already cleaned the shotgun—and pressed his fingers to the barrel and the imitation mother-of-pearl butt-plates in several places, flipped the safety off again, and put it down pointing off at an angle away from him on the other side of the table. If he'd been holding it by the barrell with oily fingers, when it went off its recoil would have kicked it over there. I had a hunch that Sheriff was a hard man to fool about guns, and I had to make it look right. I stood back and examined it.

There was one more thing, and then I was through. How many times had he shot? I stood still, trying to remember. He'd shot twice at me after the lightning flash, and then the gun had gone off when it hit the floor. So altogether there should be four cartridge cases around here on the floor. I got down on my knees and started looking. When I'd found all four, I put three of them in my pocket and stood beside the table where he was and tossed the other one in the general direction it would have gone and let it roll where it would. That left only the question of where the bullets had gone. I walked over by the bed and looked towards where I'd been when he shot. There was an open window beyond. I walked over to it. Rain was coming in. It didn't matter. If he'd shot himself in the afternoon while he was cleaning a gun he would hardly be getting up to close the windows when it started to rain in the middle of the night. I looked around the window frame and couldn't find any bullet hole, so probably they'd both gone out. The other one, when he'd dropped the gun, wasn't going to be so easy. But I was lucky. I found it in less than five minutes. It was in the baseplank next to the bed, right down by the floor. There were two thicknesses of plank here, and it hadn't gone through, so it was all right. They'd never see it.

I stood up, got the pants off the bed, put them in the purse and closed it, picked up the shoes, and stood looking at it. It was all right. It was as good as I had planned it. There was a dead man, who'd never blackmail anybody again. There was the gun he'd killed himself with because he'd forgotten a simple thing lots of others have before him but which very few people have ever forgotten twice—to check the chamber of a gun before you try to clean it.

I looked at my watch. It was two-thirty. I had plenty of time to get back to town. I hadn't forgotten anything, and I wasn't scared any more. I leaned over a little and blew out the lamp.

And then the calmness left me. I jerked my head around, listening, feeling my skin tighten up in goose-flesh. I could hear it quite plainly now, and there wasn't any doubt as to what it was.

It was an automobile horn. It went on blowing, on and on, above the monotonous sound of the rain.

19

I LOST MY HEAD for a minute. I ran out the front door and leaped off the porch, feeling the rain come pouring on to me, and then I was swallowed up in a world in which there was nothing anywhere except darkness, and water, and that unstoppable sound. It was laughing at me. It was accusing. It was pointing. Everybody on earth would hear it, and people would come from miles around to find out what was causing it and to stare at me——. It wasn't loud, because it was coming from away up on the hill, but it was like all the automobile horns in the biggest traffic jam in the world all rolled into one. I ran on blindly, unable to listen or pay any attention to the warning inside my head which was screaming for me to stop. It was insane. I had to find the road. I was running away from the house, and once I lost contact with that I'd have no place to start from. And then I tripped and fell, and that was the only thing that saved me.

It knocked a little sense into me. I lay there in the mud with the rain pouring over me, fighting to shut out that sound so I could think. Let it blow. Nobody could hear it. There wasn't another human being within miles. There wasn't anything to be afraid of in the noise itself; that was just senseless terror. The danger was in something else entirely, and if I didn't hang on to my senses and find the road I was done for.

I got up to my feet and looked behind me. I could see nothing at all. The shack could have been fifty feet back there, or it could have been a hundred miles. I tried to think, to see the whole clearing in my mind. I had run straight out the front door, so the road had to be somewhere to my left. I turned that way and started walking, feeling my way through the stumps and bushes of the clearing and fighting down that terrible yearning to run. Unless I got back on the road I didn't have a chance.

Then I felt the ruts under my feet. I had found the road. I turned right, and started running again, trying to keep between them. My breath burned in my throat, and I was cursing in a monotonous kind of frenzy. Of all the cars on the lot, I'd had to pick that one. Why in the name of God hadn't I at least asked Gulick which one it was when it cut loose on the lot Saturday afternoon? Why hadn't I had sense enough to see the warning in the way the motor had turned over when I'd started it?

I was soaked now. Water ran out of my hair and down my neck. With every step it sloshed in my shoes. Suddenly, I felt the road swerve left, and then I was out of the clearing and starting uphill through the timber. The horn didn't seem any louder as I got nearer to it. Was it getting weaker? I listened, holding my breath, but I couldn't tell. That insane urgency pulled at me, starting me running again. I missed a turn in the road and stumbled into the trees, and tripped over something and fell. The purse slipped out of my hands. I squatted on my knees and groped blindly in the mud with my free hand, afraid to let go of the shoes with the other. The sound of the horn was growing weaker. There wasn't any doubt of it. I could hear it dying. And then I could hear myself, cursing endlessly in a sort of lost and hopeless madness as I swung my hand around in the mud and water and drowned leaves, feeling for the purse. It never occurred to me I could leave it; nobody would ever find it, and there was nothing in it to identify her anyway. I had the money clasp in my pocket. I had to find it. And then my hand brushed it and it slid. I reached over and grabbed it and floundered back into the road. The pitch of the horn was changing.

I don't know how I made the last hundred yards. I was gasping, and wind was burning in my throat. I kept falling. And all the time I could hear the horn growing weaker and weaker, like an alarm clock running down. Then I was up

charles williams

to it. It was off to my left. I plunged off the road, feeling
ahead of me with my hands to get around the tree trunks. I
bumped into the car, felt my way along it to the door and
opened it, and tossed the shoes and purse inside. The horn
was still groaning faintly. I yanked the hood up and groped
around under it, jerking at wires I came in contact with and
pounding on the firewall. It stopped. I collapsed weakly on
the fender. In the sudden silence the rain sounded louder,
falling through the trees and drumming on top of the car.

Getting off the fender with an effort, I closed the hood,
and went back to the door and got in. Water ran off me on
to the seat. I switched on the ignition with shaky fingers
and reached for the starter button, weak with the unbearable suspense of it and wishing I knew how to pray. I
pushed it and the starter groaned once, coming around
until it engaged the motor, and then it stopped. I tried once
more, and there was nothing at all. The battery was dead.

I sat there for a minute slumped over the wheel listening
to the mournful sound of the rain and feeling the sick
emptiness of fear inside me. It was the thing which had
been goading me down there in the clearing and while I
was beating my brains out trying to get up the hill in the
darkness. There was no way to get the car started, and I was
at least twenty miles from town. Daybreak would catch me
long before I could walk it. And if I left the car down here
I might as well leave my card, with a note to the Sheriff.

I could see him getting his teeth into it—a man down
there who'd accidentally shot himself through the head
while I was parked here in the timber in my car because I
thought it was a drive-in movie. Now wasn't that a strange
coincidence——. I cursed, and tried to shut it off. There
must be some way out.

How long would it take me to walk it? But I knew the
answer to that. It'd take at least five hours. It'd be after eight
o'clock before I got to town. A dozen people, or twenty, or
even more, would see me, and they'd remember it. I knew
how I must look, drowned and water-soaked, covered with
mud, and my clothes torn where I'd fallen. Maybe I could
push the car back on the road, and get it started downhill to

166

crank it. I got out and felt around in the blackness to locate the trees behind it, cramped the wheels around, and went around in front. I put my shoulder against the grill, and heaved. My feet slid out from under me and I fell against the front of the car. I braced them and tried again, putting all my weight and the desperation and fear into it, and the car rolled back three or four inches, poised there, and then came back towards me. It was impossible. Four men couldn't do it. It was slightly upgrade to the road, and I couldn't do it if I tried for a week.

I'd been so near to winning. Right up to the time I'd leaned over to blow out that light I'd had the game in my hand, and now it was gone. I was done.

No, I wasn't. The idea hit me with the suddenness of light, and I straightened up, feeling the hope surge through me. Why hadn't I thought of it before? There was Sutton's car. I could drive to town in it——. No. That wouldn't do. That would still leave this one here. And how could they swallow an accidental death if his car had disappeared and turned up in town? But I was on the trail of it, and then I had it. Sutton's car was the same make. I could change batteries with him.

But how about tools? Was there anything in the car I could use to disconnect the terminals? I grabbed the keys and ran around and opened the trunk enough to get my head and shoulders under it, and began pawing wildly around inside it with my hands. There was no use even reaching for a match. They were drowned long ago. I wondered if there was any light left in the world. Maybe I had gone blind and didn't even know it. My hands bumped into something and I felt it over. It was a jack handle. And then I found the jack itself. Oh, God, I thought, there must be a pair of pliers, at least. There has to be.

Then I bumped into something and heard it rattle against the side. I groped for it and got it under my hand. My heart leaped. It was a pair of pliers. I let the door of the trunk down and went around to the battery. That terrible urgency had hold of me again, now that I could see a way out. How much longer did I have before daylight? There was no way to tell what time it was——. Sure there was. There'd be enough power in the battery to operate the lights for a few minutes. I pulled out the switch and the headlights came on very yellow and dim, and growing fainter as I looked at them. I ran around in front and looked at the watch. It was three-ten. I had to get this battery loose, walk back to the shack, get that one disconnected, and carry it back up the hill. Was there enough time?

I located the terminals. They were so covered with corrosion I couldn't even tell where the bolt nuts were. I banged savagely on them with the pliers to break it loose and twisted at them with my hands. Oh, hell, I thought in agony, if I could only see! I opened the pliers and ground them harshly around the side of the connector. And then I could feel the nut. I put the pliers on it, tightened up, and turned. Nothing gave except the pliers slipped a little, chewing up the nut. I bore down again. It came that time. The bolt broke.

It's all right, I thought crazily. It's all right. They're a press fit, and it'll work without the bolt. All I have to do is drive it on. I started gouging frenziedly at the other one. The nut turned on it, and in a few minutes I had it off. I started to lift the battery out. No, I thought. Why carry it down there? When I get the other battery I can drive down with it.

I was ready to go. I put the pliers in my pocket and groped my way through the trees to the road. I hit it and started to run when the same thought occurred to me again. I wouldn't be able to find the car when I came back. I wouldn't have the horn to guide me, and I couldn't see the handkerchief. It had probably washed away. I had to mark the place somehow. But how? Geez, I thought, I can't stand here all night. I've got to do something. I leaped to the side of the road and started sweeping my arms around. I found a small pine and broke off a limb six or seven feet long, and threw it across the ruts. I'd run into it with my feet when I came back.

I turned then and started running downhill through the

downpour, feeling the water slosh in my shoes. I lost track of the number of times I fell and how many times I blundered off the road. When I got down in the clearing and groped and stumbled my way into the yard in front of the shack, breathing was an agony, I wanted to lie down and rest. I felt my way to the car and when I got the door open I turned on the lights and held my watch under the dash. It said twelve minutes until four. I wanted to scream at it. It was lying. It hadn't taken that long.

I ground savagely at the bolts through the battery connectors, trying to work too fast and fumbling. I dropped the pliers and had to grope around for them in the darkness. Suddenly I was conscious that I was whispering to myself. I was saying, "Hurry, hurry, hurry——," in a kind of chant that had been going on forever like the rain. I got both connectors loose at last and lifted the battery out. I had to be careful about falling now. If I dropped the battery on anything solid it would break open like an over-ripe squash.

It was nothing now but sheer nightmare. I wasn't going forward any more. I was just moving my feet up and down in the same place with the same weight on my shoulders and the same rain coming down while time ran past me like a river around a snag. I couldn't remember the turns in the road. I didn't know how far I'd come, or how far I had to go. I must have passed the car. It couldn't have been this far. Maybe I'd brushed past that limb and hadn't noticed it. I'd never make it now.

And then I felt the limb against my leg. It was there. I swung off the road and started pushing my way through the trees in a frenzy to get it done, to be able to see again, and to get out of here before it was too late. And then it happened. My shoulder brushed hard against a tree trunk and it threw me off balance. The battery slipped out of my grasp and fell somewhere into the darkness ahead of me as I crashed to the ground. I heard it slam into a tree.

This was the end. It had just been teasing me all the time, and now I was really done. The battery was broken. I couldn't even find it. I lay on my stomach in the water and wet pine needles and swept my arms around, trying to

locate it and still afraid of what I'd find. My fingertips
brushed it and I slid forward and got my hands on it. It was
lying on its side. I rolled it upright and ran my hands
around it to find out if the case was broken. I couldn't tell
for sure, but it seemed to be all right. There was a hole
broken in the top of the middle cell, but both of the
terminals felt solid. Maybe it was still all right.

I picked it up and located the car. I set it on the fender,
and lifted the other battery out. It wasn't until then that I
remembered I had to get the polarity right. There wasn't
any way I could tell which was the positive and which the
negative terminal. I ran my fingers across the tops of them,
trying to feel the plus and minus markings, but I couldn't
tell because they were corroded over. There wasn't any way
on earth——. Wait, I thought. Sure there was. The positive
terminal was always larger, and the connectors would be
the same. I felt both, and I could tell which was which. I set
it in and drove the connectors down on the terminals with
the pliers, and ran around to turn on the lights. They came
up bright and strong. I looked at the watch. It was twenty
minutes after four.

I threw the other battery in, and backed out on to the
road. It was only a miracle I stayed on it at the pace I went
down the hill into the clearing. I put the battery in his car
and connected it up, working fast now with the headlights
for illumination, and as I got back in the car and turned
around the lights swept once across the bleak and lonely
cabin sitting there in the rain. I thought of him inside,
alone in the dark with his face on the table, and then I
gunned the car out of the yard, fast, and started up the hill.
I went down the other side and across the river bottom like
a man running away from hell, while the rain washed out
my tracks behind me. When I got out on the highway there
was no traffic and I rode the throttle down to the floor-
boards all the way to town.

Swinging left at the cotton gin, I circled around the way I
had before. It was still dark, but this was the dangerous part
of it now. I came up the side street and just before I swung
on to the lot I cut the headlights. I came up alongside the

last car in line and stopped and sat there for a minute before I got out. Main Street was empty in the rain.

The inside of the car was a mess from the water that had run out of my clothes, but there wasn't anything I could do about it now. I'd have to get off the lot and over to the garage the first thing when we opened, before Gulick had a chance to see it. I grabbed the purse and the shoes and got out, slipping down the street in the shadows. When I got in the alley behind the rooming house I eased through the gate and into the yard without a sound except the pounding of my heart. I hadn't seen anyone at all.

I stopped on the little porch outside my door and took off my trousers and sports shirt and wrung the water out of them, and then squeezed all I could out of the purse. Then I carried everything inside and without turning on a light felt around in the closet for my flannel robe and rolled all of it up in that. I took off the shorts and threw them in the laundry bag, and dried myself off with a towel. Using the same towel and feeling around on the floor in the dark, I mopped up what water I'd brought in with me. Then I put on some dry shorts, got a package of cigarettes out of the dresser drawer, and lay down on the bed. I looked at my watch as I lighted the cigarette. It was nearly six. It would be growing light in a few minutes. I had made it.

A little after seven I got up and shaved and dressed. It was still raining, so I got a raincoat out of the closet, picked up the bundle of stuff in the flannel robe, and carried it out to the car. I drove down and parked on the lot, and took the bundle out of the rear seat and locked it in the trunk.

As I started up the street to the restaurant I looked back under the line of cars. That was something which had been worrying me. But it was all right. The water had run, and it was just as wet under the ones that'd been there all night as under the one I'd been using.

I went on over to the restaurant. There were several people there already and they were all talking about it. It was all over town.

Harshaw was dead. He'd died a little after three that morning of another heart attack.

I COULDN'T TAKE HOLD of it at first. Why three o'clock in the morning? I ordered some breakfast and couldn't eat it. It was a rotten shame. And then I wondered why I felt so sorry about it. After all it hadn't been six hours since I'd killed a man; why should the natural death of another one bother me? I walked back to the office and just sat there looking out at the dark, miserable day. When Gulick showed up I told him he could go home. We'd close the lot and the loan office for the day, and also the day of the funeral.

Gloria came along a few minutes later. Robinson dropped her off on this side of the street and she hurried into the office. She had on a blue plastic raincoat with a hood, which made her look very pretty and young, but her face was pale and she was tired. She had already heard about Harshaw.

"Don't you think we ought to close up, Harry?" she asked.

"Yes," I said. "I've already told Gulick."

She was in the doorway, and she turned a little away from me and looked out into the street. "It's so terrible," she said quietly. She had thought the world of Harshaw.

And then I wondered if she meant Harshaw. I wanted to tell her I had her purse and shoes in the car, that there was nothing to worry about, and I couldn't. I ran right into a wall. I couldn't say a thing.

I locked the office and we went out and got in the car. I drove down the highway very slowly and we were both silent, just watching the rain. When we got to the long bridge I parked the car near the end of it and we sat there looking at the water. It was brown, and we could see the river was rising a little. They might not find him for days, I thought. If there was much more rain the road through the bottom would be impassable. Once, when there were no cars in sight in either direction, I kissed her. She drew back a little.

"It just doesn't seem right, I guess." She turned and looked out of the window.

We stayed there a half hour or longer, and I could feel the wall of silence growing up between us. I knew now why I hadn't been able to say anything back there at the office. If she couldn't talk about it, how could I? And then I suddenly realized she wasn't thinking about the shoes and purse at all, because she didn't know yet that I'd killed him. And when she did find out he was dead she would know I hadn't left them there to incriminate her. I wanted to cry out and tell her it was all right, that I knew why she'd done it and it didn't mean a thing, but how could I? I thought of the shame and the loathing she must feel, and how having to talk about it right out in the open—even to me—would crucify her, and I couldn't open my mouth. Maybe she could stand it if we didn't mention it, if we pretended it hadn't happened.

And then I thought of something else. What would it be like when they found him? Could we ever talk about it? Everything would tell her that I'd done it, but in her heart there'd always be that hope, that slim chance I hadn't as long as we didn't insist on dragging it out into the open. The whole thing was an ugly mess, and maybe the only way we'd ever be able to live with it was by ignoring it.

After a while I drove back to town. The stuff in the back of the car was still weighing on my mind, but I knew I'd have to wait until after dark to get rid of it.

"Don't you think we ought to see Mrs. Harshaw, Harry?" she asked.

"Yes," I said. "We'd better go now."

I stopped in the driveway by the side porch, and the Negro girl let us in. She said yes, Mrs. Harshaw was in and she'd see us. We went in, and she was in the living room, pale and red-eyed and dressed in a housecoat and slippers. I thought she was over-doing it a little with the weeping until I noticed she had a bad head cold. That helped her to look like the grief-stricken widow.

They had already taken him to the mortuary, and the funeral was to be on Wednesday. We expressed our sympathy and said what a fine man he'd been, and between sessions of sniffles she told us how it had happened. Apparently he had got up for something, because she had heard him out in the hall and just as she was about to call out to him and ask if anything was wrong she heard him fall. He rolled all the way down the stairs in the living room.

"Oh, it was horrible," she said pitifully, and I'd have felt sorry for her if I hadn't known better. "Going down the steps in the dark, trying to get to him, I fell myself before I got to the bottom." She slipped the housecoat down a little and showed us the bruise on her shoulder. "Somehow I got to the phone and called the doctor, but when he got here it was too late." She started crying again. She made me sick.

Well, she finally outlasted him, I thought. The whole works is hers now—probably a hundred thousand or more. I wondered if she'd sell out and leave. Probably, I thought. She could keep a whole stable of boy friends now, like a riding academy or a stud farm, and it'd work out better in a city.

Her sniffling got Gloria started. We left in a little while and I drove her home. I went back to the rooming house and tried to sleep in the afternoon, but it wasn't any good. I kept having a nightmare about trying to run uphill out of a river bottom with a dead man shackled to my leg. I'd wake up covered with sweat and shaking.

When would they find him? That was beginning to get me now. I hadn't thought about that part until now that I was getting a taste of it. *What about the waiting?* I thought everything was all right, and that they'd go for it, but how did I *know?* What if I'd forgotten something? I wouldn't know until they found him and held the inquest. Every time I thought of that cold-eyed Sheriff I'd get scared. It was going to be great. I could see that. And if it went on very long I'd be crazy.

After it was dark I drove downtown and tried to eat. My mouth was dry and everything tasted like straw. I got in the car and drove out to the abandoned sawmill, stopping on the road for a while to be sure I wasn't followed. The rain had stopped during the afternoon and now the stars were out. I parked beside the sawdust pile and got the bundle of clothes out of the trunk, went over all of it with the flashlight looking for laundry marks and cutting them out, and then carried the stuff down to the bottom of the ravine. Scooping out a hole in the bottom of the sawdust slide, I shoved them in, clothes, purse, shoes, everything, and covered them up. Then I went up a little way and started another slide. They were well buried, and as time went by more and more would fall down on them. Maybe, I thought if she stayed around here, she'd keep it sliding down. The place made me think of her, and remembering that night made me uncomfortable. Hating her didn't make any difference. Maybe that was what she'd meant by saying I'd always come back. It was so easy to remember the last time.

The funeral was Wednesday afternoon, and they still hadn't found Sutton. I couldn't seem to sleep at all now. I'd doze off for a few minutes and then wake up sweating and scared. I wondered how much longer I could take it.

Gloria and Gulick and I ordered a big floral piece for the funeral, and we all went, of course. Everybody in the county seemed to be there. Gloria cried along at the end of it, and I had to blow my nose several times myself. He was a good man, a better man than I was, even if I'd been a long time in finding it out. Gloria and I drove around afterwards, not going anywhere, and that awkward silence was still there between us. When I took her home we sat in the car a few minutes in front of the house.

"What do you suppose she'll do with the business?" she asked. "Do you think she'll sell out?"

I got what she meant, and it was the first time I'd thought of it. There'd been so much I'd overlooked that possibility of grief. If she did sell there'd be an audit of the books, and it'd probably happen before we could get all that deficit

cleaned up, even though I still had the five hundred dollars
that was in Sutton's wallet. God, I thought, how messed up
can you get?

"I don't know," I said. "She hasn't said a thing, and I
didn't want to bother her with business. But I'll see what I
can find out."

But I didn't find out anything. She didn't call up or come
around the place, and I didn't call her because I was reaching the point I couldn't think about anything except Sutton,
and when they'd find him, and what the inquest would turn
up when they did. It went on all day and all night because I
never slept more than a few minutes at a time now. In
another day or two I even quit seeing Gloria. I didn't even
call her up. I was so savage and on edge I didn't know what
I'd do or say next. By the Saturday after the funeral I
wondered if I wasn't reaching the breaking point. I began
to have an idea they'd found him and weren't saying anything, just waiting for me to crack under the strain. Maybe
they were just playing with me, and any minute one of
them would tap me on the shoulder. And then I'd get hold
of myself and I'd know this wasn't true. They just hadn't
found him yet. Nobody ever went out there. I'd just have to
wait. Wait! God, how much longer could I stand it?

It broke on Sunday morning. Two farm boys hunting
rabbits found him and came to town to report it to Tate.
Everybody was talking about it around the drugstore and
the restaurant. The Sheriff himself came over and they
went out to the oil well and were gone for a little over two
hours. When they returned, early in the afternoon, they
brought the body out and went on back to the county seat.
Nobody knew anything except what the boys had said. He
was sitting at a table, kind of bent over it, and looked like
he had been dead a long time, and they were afraid of him.
They didn't go inside the cabin.

I had to live through Sunday afternoon with nothing
more than that. I couldn't go around asking everybody I
met what they'd heard about it. I went back to my room,
but in a little while I knew I'd go crazy there. The old man
next door was reading the Bible again. I got in the car and

drove over to the county seat to a movie. It was a long picture, or maybe it was a double feature and I didn't realize it, and when I came back it was dark. There was still the night to get through. When I got back to town I went to the restaurant and forced down a little food. Tate had come back, somebody said, but he hadn't talked about it. The man died of a gunshot wound. And there'd be an inquest Monday morning. That was all.

I sat on the bed smoking cigarettes in the darkness until after three, and when fatigue caught up with me and I dozed off I began having dreams. When I shaved, I could see it on my face. I couldn't take much more. I held on to it all through Monday morning and into the afternoon, burying myself in paper work and going out on the lot now and then to go through the motions of demonstrating a car to faceless and unreal people.

I went up to the restaurant for a cup of coffee at three-thirty, and the waitress told me. She was just making conversation. She was bored, and it was something to talk about. Tate had been in. They'd held an inquest on that man, what *was* his name, the one who lived out by the oil well that had been found dead, remember—yesterday morning, wasn't it—sure it was yesterday morning because that was Sunday and she was just *dead*, that dance Saturday night, honestly—but about the man, they had held an inquest, she thought that was what Tate called it, and the man had been shot through the head with a gun, wasn't it awful, and Tate had told her the way it was——. Oh, the verdict?

It was accidental death. The man had shot himself cleaning a gun, wasn't it silly.

I never did know afterwards how I got back to the lot. All I can remember is sitting there at my desk trying to get my mind to accept the news that I had done it, that we were free of Sutton forever, and that the danger was all past. It was just too much for me to take in all at once. I'd been living with the danger and the suspense for so long I couldn't readjust that quickly.

Suddenly, I had to tell Gloria. I wanted to call her on the

phone. I'd been avoiding her because of the pressure I was under, and now I wanted to see her and start making up for it. Then I stopped. What was I going to tell her? Sutton was something we didn't talk about. And certainly not over the phone. But I wanted to call her anyway, and make a date to see her that night. We could go on now. Everything would be just the way it had been before, and somehow we'd break down that wall that had grown up between us. Some way I could make her understand it didn't matter. But I wouldn't call her; she was just across the street, and I wanted to see her. I had started out the door when the phone rang.

"Mr. Madox?" the voice said when I picked up the receiver. It was Dolores Harshaw.

"Yes," I said.

"I'm sorry I haven't called before, but I'm sure you'll understand. I wanted to thank you for the flowers and for being so kind, and all. It was very nice of all of you." She paused. Now, what the hell, I thought. Why so goody-goody? There must be somebody in the room with her, one of the neighbours, or the maid.

"Why, that's all right," I said. "It was the least we could do."

"Well, it was awful nice. But what I wanted to talk to you about was the business. I know you've been wonderful about it; what my plans were, I mean. Do you think you could come over tonight, say around seven, so we could discuss it, you and Miss Harper both, I mean?"

"Sure," I said. "I'll tell her. We were wondering about it, as a matter of fact, but we didn't want to bother you. Are you planning to sell out? Is that it?"

"Oh, no. I guess from what the lawyers say it'll take some time for the whole thing to be settled, but I wouldn't sell out anyway. I think I should try to carry it on—for George's sake, you know. And of course I'll want you and Miss Harper to go right on the way you have been. I'm sure it couldn't be in better hands."

There must be a dozen people in the room, I thought. She hadn't even thrown in a nasty dig at Gloria just for old times' sake. Maybe she'd decided to become a social leader, and pull down the shades before she turned in with her boy friends. Well, I didn't care a damn what she did, as long as she paid my salary.

After she had hung up I sat there a few minutes letting it soak in before I called Gloria. It was wonderful to tell her.

I picked her up that evening and we started over. I thought of how much it was like that other time, when Harshaw had asked us to come over. And afterwards we could go out to the river, as we had then, and I could take her face in my hands and kiss her and we could break through to each other again. We would start all over. The past was gone. Sutton didn't matter any more. I could make her see that. I knew I could.

She broke in on my thoughts. "Harry," she said, "there's something I've got to tell you. I've been trying to all week, but I want to tell you now."

"We'll go somewhere afterwards and talk," I said. "Then you can tell me, if you think you have to."

"Yes. I have to. It's about Sutton."

I stared ahead into the lights, trying to keep my face still. "Sutton's dead. Nothing matters about him any more. Nothing at all. You believe me, don't you, honey, that it doesn't matter now?"

"This does, Harry. I've got to tell you. You see, I thought all week that he had gone away. Because——. Well, you see, I gave him that five hundred dollars. After you told me not to. I took it out there and begged him to leave. So now it's going to take us that much longer——."

I reached out and patted her hand. "It's all right," I said. "It doesn't make any difference."

It was a strange thing for her to say, I thought. Why bring up that one part of the whole mess, if we were going to ignore it? I should have got it then, but I didn't, for we were turning in the driveway and I didn't think about it any more. I stopped by the side porch and we got out. The light was on and as we rang the bell and stood there waiting I looked at her, thinking how pretty she was. She had on a yellow summer dress with big fluffy bows or something on the shoulders, and her stockings were some dark shade. She seemed to like dark-coloured nylons———.

I was staring. I couldn't say anything, and the skin on the back of my neck was tightening up into gooseflesh like frozen sandpaper. I got it now, when it was forever too late.

It was what she was wearing on her feet. They were wedgies. They were wedgies with grass straps.

21

D<small>OLORES HARSHAW CAME</small> to the door then and let us in. I was
numb. I was operating on pure reflex, trying to keep going
and cover up. Somewhere far off I could hear them giving it
the how-nice-you-look and what-a-lovely-dress routine
while the wreckage fell all around me and I could see what
I had done. There was no escape. There wasn't any way to
go back, so all I could do was walk the rest of the way into
it and pray. It was all dangerous now, and I knew it, but I
wondered if she did. We were standing hip-deep in gunpowder and she might not have any more sense than to
reach for a match. I'd killed Sutton, and she was the only
one on earth who knew it. Did she realize what that meant?
All the time I'd thought it was Gloria, and Gloria didn't
know anything. She was standing there in the magazine
with us, and no matter what happened I had to be sure she
was out before it blew up.

There was too much of it and it was coming at me too
fast to see the whole picture at once. Crazy pieces of it kept
flashing up in the sick confusion of my thoughts, and then
they'd be gone and there'd be something else. There was
Harshaw. I didn't have to wonder any more why he'd had a
heart attack and fallen down the stairs at a crazy hour like
that. Had he just happened to catch her coming in at three
in the morning barefoot and naked except for a dress half
torn off by the underbrush and stuck to her with the rain,
or had she done it deliberately? Nobody would ever know,
and they couldn't touch her. Maybe he had given her that
bruise on the shoulder, or maybe she'd got it when she fell
over us back there in the shack. But what difference did it
make? She knew I'd killed Sutton and I had to shut her up,
but how?

And now I knew why Sutton had waited all that time to put the squeeze on me. He hadn't even been there at the fire; or at least he hadn't seen me. She'd told him. When I'd given her the brush-off, she'd merely gone back to him, and because there wasn't any other way to get even with me she'd told him the whole thing. And now he was dead because he thought he could cash in on it, and she knew I'd killed him, and why.

"Don't you feel well, Mr. Madox?"

I tried to come out of it. She was looking at me with the dead-pan innocence of a baby. All the ash-blonde curls were burnished and glinting in the lamplight, and the shiny black dress looked as if it had been packed by hand. She was in deep mourning from the skin out and laughing inside like a cat up to its whiskers in cream. I'd given her the brush, and now she could hang me. All she had to do was pick up the phone and call the Sheriff.

Is she stupid, or what? I thought. Doesn't she know I'll kill her? But then I knew the answer to that, too. She wasn't stupid. She'd asked Gloria to come, hadn't she?

"Oh," I said. "I'm all right. I feel fine."

There was nothing showing on the surface. Gloria couldn't suspect anything at all. We went over and sat down, Gloria in a big chair and I on the sofa across from her, while Dolores Harshaw leaned back in a platform rocker. We were all grouped around the coffee table.

"I know you've been wondering," Dolores said, "I mean, about the business. I would have called you sooner, but it's been such a blow, you know——."

She went on giving us the brave little widow bearing up under everything. I didn't pay any attention to it. I was too busy with the physical strain of keeping my face from showing anything and trying to find the answer to the question that went around and around in my mind in a kind of endless nightmare. *What was she going to do?*

I could hear her voice going on, like a radio in a burning house. "—what poor George would have wanted. He thought a great deal of both of you. So of course I couldn't sell out. I'm going to try to carry on just the same."

She had the rope around my neck, and when she got ready she'd drop the trap. With Gloria here I was helpless. And she knew that, of course, so whatever it was it was going to be done now, before we left and I got a chance to get her alone.

She was picking up an envelope which was lying on the coffee table. "It must have been terrible," she went on, "because I think he knew in his heart it might happen any time. Ever since we came back from Galveston he had a little notebook that stayed right by his side all the time, and he kept writing down his ideas about the business and the things he wanted to be sure would be carried on just——" Her voice broke a little. She was tremendous as the brave little widow. She gathered herself up with a pitiful smile and went on. "—just in case it did happen. I've written it all out, and I thought Mr. Madox should read it, since he'll be in charge. And of course you too, Miss Harper, if he thinks you should."

She handed it over to me. There was nothing in her face but that same dead-pan innocence. Gloria was watching her, and then me, with only polite curiosity. She probably thought she'd been working for Harshaw long enough to know his politics.

I opened the envelope and slid it out. It was a carbon copy, two pages single-spaced on a typewriter. I looked at the heading of it, and I knew where the original was. It was in a safe-deposit box somewhere or in some lawyer's office, where I'd never get to it. And I knew that I wasn't going to kill her. As long as both of us lived, the safest place she would ever be was with me, and I was going to hope she went on living for a long, long time.

"This statement is to be turned over to the District Attorney's office after my death," it began, and she had it all there. She hadn't left out a thing. She admitted lying about my being there at the fire right after it broke out, and described the way I had driven up and hurried into the crowd thirty minutes later. She told them about my having been in the building before, and how she had told Sutton all of this, and of her recognizing me in the lightning flash

when the storm broke that night. The clincher was at the
end, and it was something I hadn't known before. She'd
gone back down there just after daybreak, after the doctor
had left the house. She had to know what had happened,
because her purse and things were there. And when she
found Sutton dead and the purse gone she had it all.

I read it all the way through, cold as ice and seeing the
walls rise up around me. I could quit looking for a way out.
There wasn't any. As long as she was living she could turn
me in any time she felt like it, and the minute she died of
anything at all they'd have that statement. It wasn't wit-
nessed, of course, and maybe it wasn't legal, but it didn't
have to be. It put the finger on me, and the weight of all the
other evidence would be overwhelming. They'd get it out of
me. Of course, if she turned it over to them while she was
still alive, she might be in trouble herself—but that was a
laugh, or would have been if I hadn't felt more like screaming. I'd go to the electric chair, and she might get a few
months' suspended sentence.

I folded it up very slowly and slipped it back in the envelope while they watched me. I couldn't say anything. I
didn't trust my voice. Somehow I managed to keep my face
utterly blank as I dropped it on the coffee table and looked
at her. She had me and she knew it. I waited.

And then she let me have it, without saying a word to
me. She was talking to Gloria.

She leaned back in her chair and lighted a cigarette. She
was friendly, and quite sympathetic. "Now, about the
shortage in your accounts, Miss Harper," she said. "I know
you'll understand that Mr. Madox was only doing what he
believed was right when he told me about it. And of course
I wouldn't think of bringing charges. You can continue
right on the way you have been until it's all taken care of,
and you'll still have your job afterwards if you want it. I
want you to know, dear, that we're your friends, and that he
hated having to do it as much as I hate having to mention
it now. And he insisted that you be given another
chance——."

That was the end, and that was the way she did it. Just

one clean swing of the axe. And it was something I hadn't even thought of. She had told Sutton about me, and then Sutton had told her. They must have had a wonderful time. And I'd had them both dead to rights in the shack that night, and had let her get away. I didn't want to think about it. I'd go crazy.

Gloria sat straight upright in her chair, saying nothing, and when she turned to look at me her face was pale and her eyes were unbelieving and they were waiting for me to say something, anything at all, even one word, or to say it with my eyes if I couldn't open my mouth, and then after a long time she quit waiting and turned her face away. It was very simple. I had just watched myself die.

I didn't have to let her believe it, of course. After all, I had a choice. I had a lovely choice. I could have told her the truth.

She was magnificent. I think I loved her more at that moment than I ever had before, but maybe it was just because she was gone forever now and I was thinking about that. She got up with her face very still and controlled, and said politely, "Yes, I understand, Mrs. Harshaw. And of course it will all be paid back. So if there isn't anything else, you don't mind if I go now, do you?"

Dolores got up and said sweetly, "Of course not, dear."

Before I thought, I stood up. "Wait," I said. "I—I'll drive you home."

"Thank you," she said, looking at the place I would have been standing if I had existed. "I'll walk."

She went out, and the screen door closed behind her, and I heard her going down the steps and along the gravel of the drive.

After her steps had died away there was silence in the room and I turned around and looked at this woman I was tied to for as long as I could go on living. She was leaning back in the platform rocker with her legs crossed and one foot swinging, and she was smiling.

"Harry, darling," she said, "I don't think you'll ever have much luck explaining to her."

I thought of how near I had been to winning, every step

of the way, and how I'd just missed it every time because of her. I could have stopped Sutton without killing him if she hadn't told him about the bank, because Sutton was afraid of me until he had that. And if she hadn't been there in the shack that night, if I'd sense enough to know it had to be her——. I thought of Gloria walking home alone in the dark believing that I had sold her out for this sexy tubful of guts and her money, believing it and forever, because I could never tell her.

The room was filling with that same red mist there'd been that night I'd killed Sutton. What did it matter now if they sent me to the chair? I'd lost it all. I'd lost everything because of her. I walked slowly over and stood looking down at the sensuous and slightly mocking face and the white column of her throat.

"You'll have to beg now," she said. "You had your chance, but you threw it away because you wanted that little owl. I'm going to enjoy hearing you beg me to marry you. You see, you have to look after me, Harry. Something might happen to me——."

"Yes," I said. "Something might."

Maybe she heard the murder in my voice, because she quit smiling and her eyes went wide. I reached down and caught the front of the black dress. It ripped loose at her belly and everything from there on up came off in my hand, but she came up out of the chair with the force of it and stood there swaying, the scream beginning and then chopping suddenly off as I put my right hand on her throat and threw her across the coffee table on to the sofa. I went across it after her just as she wiggled off the sofa on to the floor, still trying to get her breath to scream, and then I was on her. I got both hands on her throat and there was nothing inside me but the black madness of that desire to kill her, to close my hands until she turned purple and lay still and there'd be an end to her forever. Let them send me to the chair. Let 'em burn me. All they could do was kill me——.

It's like committing suicide by holding your breath.

I relaxed my hands and turned her loose.

"You see, Harry," she said. She looked down at the wreckage of her clothing and the big, spread-out breasts, and then at me, and smiled. She'd been right the first time, and she knew it.

"Kiss me," she said.

"Yes," I said. We were lying against the edge of the sofa and her hair was mussed and she was half naked and I could smell the perfume she always wore.

The smile broadened and she put her arms up around my neck. "Yes, what?"

I knew the answer now.

"Yes, dear," I said.

That was almost a year ago. We're married now, and I go to work every morning at nine, and sell cars, and lend money, and make more than I know what to do with. I belong to the Chamber of Commerce, and the service clubs, and even the Volunteer Fire Department. I like to think that some day I might be a director of the bank, because that would be the final, supreme laugh of them all when I'm lying awake at night. It's something to look forward to—not much, but something—and maybe some day I'll make it and become the only bank director in the world who started at the bottom by robbing the bank and worked his way up by becoming indispensable to a bitch, and the only one anywhere who has twelve thousand three hundred dollars of his bank's assets buried under six inches of slowly rotting manure in a collapsing barn on a sandhill and who intends to let it stay there until the barn rots and the money rots and he rots himself, because if he ever dug it up and looked at it he'd go crazy and kill himself. It's an ambition, and everybody should have one, even if it's only a good laugh in the middle of the night when he has a little trouble getting to sleep because he's worrying about his wife. She might be tiring of him, or catching cold.

I've given up trying to find out where the original of that statement is, and I know I'll never get my hands on it, the same as I know I'll never have the nerve to take a chance and run. Of course she probably wouldn't do anything. A dozen times I've almost made it. I get in the car and think that all I have to do is drive, and keep on driving, and the chances are she wouldn't do a thing. Why should she? She'd only get herself in trouble for abetting a crime and withholding evidence, and I'd be gone, and when they did get me back all she'd have would be a corpse with a shaved spot on his head and a couple of them on his arms, and that wouldn't be of much use to a woman who needs them living.

I know a way to make her talk, and I've tried it twice, and asked her, and she told me everything except where that statement is, and I know that if she wouldn't tell me then she'll never tell me. It was a good idea, but it didn't work, and I'll never try it any more because the second time she stopped right in the middle of gasping, "Oh, God, please, please, darling, please," and got out of bed and went downstairs naked and when she came back holding her hands behind her I didn't know it was an ice-pick she had until she had put it through my neck. It went in a little off centre and missed the jugular vein by a good three-quarters of an inch, and came out under my ear. A little iodine fixed it up and it didn't even get infected, but I never tried that again. She was in a position of strength, as lawyers say, and she wouldn't tolerate work stoppage or breach of contract in mid-term.

She did tell me about the silver money clasp. When Gloria went out there in the afternoon she had the five hundred dollars in it, and when Sutton saw it he demanded it as well as the money. And then he told Dolores about it, and showed it to her, and she wanted it. He wouldn't give it to her, though, and she'd left it lying there on the table, intending to slip it into her purse when he wasn't looking. And if I hadn't just happened to pull the purse around that final inch, looking behind it for the ash-tray—but I never go much beyond that with it. You can take just so much might-have-been.

She'd been really scared, of course, when she went back a little after daylight that morning to get her stuff and found Sutton dead. She knew, because the stuff was gone, that I'd found the money clasp and thought it was Gloria, but she also knew I'd get wise to my mistake sooner or later, and that I'd have to kill her to cover it up. So she had written out that statement as soon as she got back to the house, plus a letter to the lawyers to tell them where to find it—along with her will—in case of her death. The only thing she had to do then was to make sure I read a copy of it before I got my hands on her.

Gloria had no choice but to believe what she told her. After all, I didn't deny it. She gave me every chance to say it wasn't true, and I couldn't even look at her. And to make it worse she already knew I had changed somehow and even seemed to avoid her from the very night Harshaw died. Naturally, she had no way of knowing it was also the night Sutton died, and that he was what was on my mind, and I couldn't tell her.

Not that I know what she really thinks, or that I'll ever know. We work together from nine until five and she is very efficient and does a beautiful job and she says, "Yes, Mr. Madox," and "No, Mr. Madox," and in her eyes there's nothing but polite reserve and behind that nothing but blankness, an impenetrable wall of it. Beyond that——. Who knows? Maybe there's no feeling at all, not even contempt. Probably there's only a big calendar pad of so many months, so many more weeks, and days, and hours, that she has left ahead of her until she can put the last penny back and balance the books and be free.

And I can't even help her. I've got plenty of money, enough to put it all back at once, and I love her enough to want to give her the only thing she probably lives for—the day she can tear the last page off that calendar and go away forever—and I can't shorten her sentence one day. Dolores knows too well just how much is left and how long it will take. But even if I could help her, she wouldn't accept it. It's something she has to do.

But that still isn't the terrible part of it, the thing that will drive me crazy some night if I don't find some way to quit thinking about it. The final, ghastly joke of the whole thing is that she's paying back five hundred dollars *she doesn't even owe*, and there isn't any way in the world I can tell her. It's the five hundred I took out of Sutton's wallet that night. So how can I stop her?

But in the final analysis her sentence will soon be over, and I'm the one who is doing life. In a little over two months now she'll be free and can walk out of the office for the last time and go on with a life of her own. I think she and Eddie Something date a lot now that he's home from college, and nothing is hopeless or irrevocable when you're twenty-one. I'm the one who couldn't make it. I had a try-out in the big leagues, but I didn't have the stuff, and they sent me back. I've found my own level again, and I'm living with it.

Maybe it'll be better when she's gone, and maybe it'll be worse. At least I get to see her now. I ask her if she knows where this paper is, or that paper, and she says, "Yes, Mr. Madox," and I look at her, thinking of that morning a little less than a year ago, in this same office, when I saw her for the first time, very fresh and lovely and looking like a long-stemmed yellow rose, and I have to fight down that almost unbearable longing to cry out to her and ask her if she ever thinks of it, or remembers it, or the day Spunky was lost and I held her face in my hands and kissed her, or the night on the bridge when she said she loved me.

But I never ask it. There's no need to, because I know what she would say.

"No, Mr. Madox."

About the Author

Charles Williams was born in Texas in 1909. After growing up in Texas and New Mexico, he worked as a merchant seaman and, during the Second World War, joined the U.S. Navy.

His first novel, *Hill Girl*, was published in 1950. In all, he wrote twenty-one novels, of which all but two can be classified in the suspense genre. Fourteen of these books were sold to the movies, including *The Hot Spot*, which was released in 1990.

Mr. Williams died in 1975.